CAPTAIN ZERO:
CITY OF DEADLY SLEEP

CITY OF
DEADLY SLEEP

By G. T. Fleming–Roberts

STEEGER BOOKS • 2020

PUBLISHING HISTORY

"City of Deadly Sleep" originally appeared in the November 1949 (Vol. 1, No. 1) issue of *Captain Zero* magazine. Copyright © 1949 by Popular Publications, Inc. Copyright renewed © 1977 and assigned to Steeger Properties, LLC. All rights reserved.

CHAPTER 1
THE VOICE FROM HELL

MANNING FELT like laughing, but there was no laughter in him. He sat there in the cramped 'phone booth, the sweat oozing out onto his tanned face. It dripped off him onto his white palm beach jacket. His restless gray eyes roved about the barroom outside the 'phone booth. He could see a blur of faces out there, but not one of them was watching him.

He turned back to the 'phone, his mouth twitching.

"Say that again. I don't understand at all. What's the gag?"

The voice spoke again. It was no ordinary voice, this one. It had a metallic, penetrating timbre, a resonant quality that set it apart from all other voices. In some ways it was not a human voice at all. Its vibrations sent chills creeping over Manning's flesh. If the voice of doom had called him up on the 'phone, it would say these very words.

"Get yourself a gun, Manning," the voice said. *"Carry it with you wherever you go. You may be number three."*

The chills spread along Manning's spine again. He grinned with his lips, a humorless, arid grin. His mouth cracked and his throat was dry. He eased back against the edge of the 'phone booth and loosened his tie. He pulled it away from his constricted throat. The heat in the booth weighed heavily on him.

"Who the hell are you? Let me in on the very funny joke, pal."

1

Akara fired, and the gun, which had no visible means of support, leaped, and whirled in the air.

There was a thoughtful pause. Tension built in George Manning's chest. He could not breathe.

The penetrating, dread-laden voice spoke again. *"No funny gag, Manning. First it was Sam Irwin. Then it was Bill Cordray. Number three may be you. Get a gun—use it. That is all I can say."*

Manning licked his lips and stared at the receiver. He was about to speak, but a dull metallic click came over the wire. The other party had hung up.

Manning slowly put the receiver back and sat in the booth, letting the cold, icy sweat drain off him onto his clothes. He straightened his neatly arranged tie once again and got up.

Sam Irwin and Bill Cordray.

Cordray he had known vaguely—back as far as college. Irwin not so well at all. But there was one thing about them both he did know. They were dead. They had been killed—murdered. One, two, and George Manning might be number three.

Manning looked down at his long brown hands. He forced a grin. A gag. A funny gag and pretty soon a couple jerks would come up to Manning's table and slap him on the back and laugh their beery breaths in his face. And he would try to laugh too.

He opened the 'phone booth door and walked out into the dimly lit bar of the Purple Cat roadhouse. The faint purple lights hit him obliquely, painting his tanned skin a deep gold-brown hue. In his white palm beach jacket he looked like a moving picture negative as he walked along in the purple lights.

Glancing carefully about him, he moved across the bar to his table. No one in the place looked like a gunman. Not that Manning would know a gunman if he did see one—unless maybe they were like the bouncers at Pete Flosso's place. Or the plug-uglies at Johnny Akara's.

No. Everything looked the same as ever.

Irwin and Cordray, Manning thought. Lined with plenty of gilt-edged bonds, each one of them. And so, Manning thought ruefully, was George Manning II. It was not so damned funny.

"Hi baby," he smiled absently at the violet-eyed girl sitting at his table. She watched him as he sat down. She leaned forward, her orange hair glinting dead in the phony bar light. Her eyes were slitted and worried.

"Who was that, big boy? The wife? She suspect something?"

"Nuts," said Manning, lifting his glass of scotch and water. "Nuts to Gertrude. Okay?"

The girl laid a hand on his wrist. "Yeah, yeah," she said. "I didn't mean nothing by it. But I'm interested in snoopers, big boy. Guys following around taking notes down in pads. I'm telling you, big boy, I'm decent. I ain't just one of them pick-ups. I got decency if I got nothing else."

Manning smiled. His eyes were flat and dead. "Sure, baby." He couldn't even remember her name. Gloria? Helene with a long *ee?* "No, you ain't one of them pick-ups. You're a sweet kid and I'm the luckiest guy around this town tonight."

She drew her hand back, sitting stiff in her chair. "You shut up with that smart talk, Mr. Manning. I got boy friends. I can pick and choose. Anyway, I didn't want to come here. You dragged me. I was all set for Flosso's place on the bluffs, but you had to get smart and tell me no dice—"

Manning's eyes slitted. "Shut up," he said quietly.

She drew herself up again. "You go to hell."

Manning flipped a fiver out onto the table and stood up, his eyes burning bright. "Come on, baby. I'm taking you home. I'm a funny guy. I can take so much. But then all of a sudden I can't take any more."

She sneered. "You ain't even got a car to drive me home in, Mr. Manning! I ain't leaving for no taxi ride with you. I got boy friends. I come out for a good time and—"

Manning was halfway to the entrance when she looked up. Her eyes widened and her mouth sagged open. She started to hurl herself up around the table after him, but her eye lit on the five spot. She made a fast calculation and sat down again. She turned around with a smile and looked over the crowd There were plenty of suckers out tonight...

MANNING STOOD in front of the Purple Cat, watching the heat lightning race back and forth across the sky to the west. It would rain later that night. The summer sky would split apart and the water would come down in buckets. The humid heaviness in the air weighed on the earth about him, pushing down like a strange brooding evil.

That damned voice. Funny thing. Unnerving. Odd. Otherworldly. And what it said—*"Look out. You may be number three."* Strange. If somebody was going to kill him—the way Irwin and Cordray had been killed—why warn him? Why put him on guard? Why speak with the phony voice? Why not come right out in the open and tell him man to man? Why the big vaudeville act?

It didn't figure, any way you looked at it.

Manning lit a cigarette. Its flame illuminated the golden tan of his face, the steady gray eyes, the deft chin. He was in his late thirties, George Manning. And even in all that time he had not been able to go through the family fortune—yet. He'd tried—Lord, he'd tried. But there was so damned much of it.

He chuckled. Give him another ten years. He'd piddle it all away on those fancy roulette wheels in Pete Flosso's Moon River Casino. That smooth, greasy Flosso. Hell, people who didn't have money never knew how hard it was to get rid of it sometimes. The stuff just stuck to your fingers. Even the gambling went well part of the time. Them as has, gets.

The highway stretched back across flat plains, and east back to the city of Pendleville. A walk in the fresh air might clear out the cobwebs in his head—he was sleepy and dizzy from alcohol fumes and the smell of cheap perfume.

Manning took a deep drag off his cigarette and started moving along the gravel shoulder of the highway. Maybe he'd thumb a ride into town. The cops had confiscated his driver's license a week ago when he'd smashed a vegetable vendor's cart on Vine Street. The judge had given him a temperance lecture. You'd think Manning couldn't hold his liquor as well as the next man. Hell, that was the first thing a Manning learned in life.

Irwin and Cordray.

Manning remembered the newspaper story he had seen on Irwin's death in the *Daily World.*

SAMUEL IRWIN, JR. VICTIM OF ASSAULT

June 14. The body of Samuel Irwin, Jr., 23, son of one of Pendleville's most prominent citizens, was found in a vacant lot near the Irwin home early this morning by Robert Brister, employee of Curtiss Creamery.

Young Irwin had suffered repeated blows from a blunt instrument about the face and head. He died as a result of a skull fracture, according to Coroner Ralph Bindwood.

Police hare discarded robbery as a motive, since over two hundred dollars in cash was found on Irwin's person....

That was Irwin.

Cordray's body, on the other hand, had been found just inside the city limits, on the shoulder of the state highway, flat on his face in front of his own car, one bullet through the left lung and another through the back of his head.

One, two, and....

Manning grinned. They couldn't kill him—he didn't even have his car to get around in. How could they follow his car if it was parked safe in his garage?

Anyway, why would anybody want to murder him? He didn't owe any money. He'd never hurt anybody. He was a hell of a nice guy. He had a good family. Who had it in for George Manning II?

The whole thing was pretty silly.

"Well, Manning, I see you had to play bright boy tonight and disregard my warning, didn't you?" The voice startled him, coming as it did out of thin air.

MANNING STOPPED. He drew the cigarette out of his mouth and stared stupidly in front of him into the black darkness of the highway. But there was no one there at all. No one.

From the highway to the nearest clump of brush was a ten foot stretch. And the voice had come from directly in front of him!

He turned around. There was no one in back of him. He could see the deserted highway and the bare gravel shoulder all the way back to the roadhouse. In the distance the Purple Cat light blinked on and off.

Manning faced the voice again. It was that strange, other-worldly penetrating voice—the same voice that had spoken to him on the telephone, the voice of omniscience, the voice of eternity.

"Who the hell are you?" Manning gasped out, his cheek twitching. "It's a gag, and it's a good one. What do you want?"

The voice paused. Then it spoke again, reassuringly, unemotionally. *"I told you to get a gun, Manning, Your life is in great danger, I'm only trying to help you."*

Manning sucked on his cigarette. The red glow painted his face a moment. He stared ahead of him coldly, his eyes focused on the spot the voice had come from.

"What the devil do you want? Is this a blackmail shake-down? If it is, it's a good one. I thought I was going nuts."

The voice smiled, tolerantly, kindly. *"No blackmail, Manning. I'm trying to help you, if you will only let me."*

"Why didn't you help Bill Cordray, if you're such hot stuff on the crystal ball?"

The voice said sadly: *"I didn't know in time—about Irwin and Cordray. But now I do know—see the pattern. You may be next, Manning. Get a gun!"*

Manning bit his lip. "Who are you?"

The voice smiled. *"They call me Captain Zero. You have never heard of me. Not many people have, yet. But they will."*

Manning smiled sardonically. "What do you want, Zero? Money? Payment for the tip?"

"No, Manning. I want your promise. Buy a gun. You're going to need it. I can't help you—but I can warn you."

The burning tip of Manning's cigarette bit into his finger. He snapped the butt forward involuntarily, the spark arcing ahead. Then, suddenly, in midair, the cigarette butt reversed direction, bouncing back down onto the pavement at Manning's feet.

Manning's eyes stared, his jaw dropped open. It was almost as if the cigarette had struck some unseen barrier, and had bounced off it. There was somebody there—hiding in a trick garment!

Manning moved forward, his hands extended outward. Laughter sounded from the spot the voice had spoken. Sardonic, resonant laughter. Manning's groping hands touched something alive—it was flesh! And suddenly, as he stood there, crouched, the sweat sliding down his face and arms, he felt himself gripped around the wrist by a solid, tight pressure—the pressure of live, muscled hands—*that he could not see!*

Instinctively, Manning drew back, pulling himself away from the thing—whatever it might be. But now the invisible hand had him, and it would not let him go. Gasping, Manning shot a fist out toward the unseen figure, flailing his arms desperately.

The laughter went on. Manning felt himself jerked downward. Something knotted up under him, and he flipped head over heels onto the pavement. Stunned, he lay there, too astonished to move. Above him he could hear the laughter.

"Maybe you will listen to me now, my friend. Irwin and Cordray were gamblers. The other night you lost money to Pete Flosso. Manning, arm yourself. You, like them, may die, too."

In the distance Manning could hear the hum of an approaching car motor. It came from the highway behind him. Thank God! Somebody would stop. He could get away from this strange, terrifying thing. He tensed himself together, leaped to his feet.

"Manning," cried the voice, surprised.

Manning stumbled on down the pavement, reeling back and forth in his flight. He could hear soft footsteps catting up behind him. Manning ran faster, the gravel crunching under his own feet. Then the icy-cold, fleshy grip tightened onto his shoulder, spinning him sideways.

With a savage twist and a violent thrust of his shoulders, Manning hurled the invisible force off him, and sent it pitching down the embankment toward the brush that lined the highway gulley. He could hear the crashing of rocks below and the snapping of brush. Then silence.

BLINDING HEADLIGHTS cut into the darkness and the automobile came into sight. Manning ran out into the middle of the highway, waving his arms about. In the gulley there was a sudden start. Stones slid about.

"Manning!" shouted the voice from the gulley. *"No! Not that car!"* There was a sudden scramble of rocks and the invisible thing clambered up onto the gravel shoulder.

The automobile—it was a taxi—screeched to a stop, and Manning yanked the door open wildly. He hurtled himself into

11

the back seat, slamming the door shut behind him. Instantly he heard the handle turning and twisting from the outside.

The door jerked open. Manning tore at the handle again, hardly knowing what he was doing in his blind, paralyzing fear. He pulled at it with all the strength in his body.

"Start the car!" yelled Manning. "For Pete's sake—start the car! Anywhere! Get out of here!"

The taxi dug out with the sound of tearing rubber and pavement. It leaped into the air, and then bounced ahead on the pavement. Suddenly the handle gave and the door pulled to. There was no more tugging from outside and the taxi drove on.

Manning leaned back against the cushions, exhausted. He was shaking from head to foot. His palm beach suit was torn and sweaty and greasy. But there was no blood on it.

I must be going nuts, Manning gasped. I must have imagined all that.

Lightning shivered across the horizon, and Manning could see a jagged line of trees, a barn, a pasture. He looked ahead of him at the driver, and he could see his stolid silhouette. A pair of broad shoulders rose slightly above the back of the seat, then a thick, short neck, and a head that was wide between two big ears. The head appeared flat on top because of the cap.

Manning looked at the headboard of the car. There wasn't any license. There wasn't any meter, either. It was a bootleg hack. Hell, that was all right. Wildcat or legit, it had saved his neck tonight.

Manning looked ahead into the highway, through the windshield. The big beams of the headlights swept through the blackness. A narrow iron bridge rushed into the headlights. A narrow iron bridge. Where had he read about a narrow iron bridge...?

"Say!" Manning said abruptly, leaning forward, jabbing a couple of fingers into the driver's back. "Where are we going, driver?"

The driver half turned. "Anywhere. You said anywhere."

"Um," Manning said. "Listen. Isn't this the road where they found Cordray's body?"

The car slowed down. "Who'd you say?" The driver's voice was tight.

"Bill Cordray."

"Never heard of him." The driver let his breath slide out and stepped on the accelerator.

Manning leaned back, watching the darkness slide by. "What's your name?" he asked the driver.

"Joe," said the driver.

"Joe, you must have read about Cordray in the papers. They found him around here somewhere, along the road, shot in the back."

"Oh, *that* guy. Naw, that was clear over on the other side of town."

"No, no. This side. Past the bridge. I'll bet you twenty bucks. If you'll slow down, I'll show you."

Manning felt the drag of the brakes. He stared out at the dark. "Right up here somewhere," he said. "I'll swear it was right around here. I remember reading about it."

Joe brought the car to a complete stop. "Maybe I just lost twenty bucks," Joe said. "Maybe this is it. I'll look and see.

There'll be marks on the road." Manning watched Joe get out, saw his short stalky figure in the light, the brown tropic worsted suit that Joe wore, the polished yellow-brown oxfords.

He watched Joe move forward and stop just off the road shoulder, his back to the car. Joe put a hand up and beckoned. He pointed down at the crushed gravel on the road shoulder.

Manning got out. "What've you got there, Joe?"

"Bloodstains," Joe said as Manning moved past him.

"Where?" Manning looked at the gravel, and it was as white as any he had ever seen. "I don't see any." He turned, glancing up, looking into the glare of the headlights, saw Joe pointing, not at the crushed rock at all but at Manning.

Pointing a gun at Manning, a gun that looked like a cannon.

Manning took a faltering backward step, thinking of the warning voice he had heard, thinking of Irwin and Cordray, thinking of everything that had ever happened to him in all his life—everything that had meaning and reason, and this had no meaning or reason at all.

"No, Joe! For God's sake—!"

The gun jerked, and blotted itself out in an orange-red explosion of flame that mushroomed out like a big sun from the muzzle of the gun. The two shots came so close together that they sounded like one.

Manning stumbled forward, fell onto his stomach, kicking at the gravel that layered the road shoulder. A puff of white dust rose from his shoes into the headlight beams.

"You may be number three!" He remembered the words in

14

the blinding, numbing instant, and his mouth twitched wryly. Number three in a series of what?

Before he had any reasonable answer to that question, he was dead.

CHAPTER 2
JOHNNY THE TURK

IT WAS all in his mind, Joe kept telling himself. The wheel was not actually sticky. Or if it was sticky, that was because of the sweat on his hands. Sweat—not blood.

Once there had been blood, and he'd got it first on his hands and then on the steering wheel. That was the first time. Irwin. He'd beaten Irwin with a short hunk of lead pipe, and he'd gotten blood on his hands. Even after repeated washings, he had felt its stickiness.

Joe took one hand from the wheel and tried to get a look at his palm from the glow of the dash. No blood. Clenching the hand, he still felt its stickiness.

He said, "Hell!"

The narrow iron bridge loomed in the headlights, and Joe tramped on the brake pedal—yielding to an impulse to get out and wash his hands. But when he realized the danger of stopping so close to the scene of the murder, he stepped on the gas in a sudden burst that swept him across the bridge.

"Slow down!" he told himself aloud, fiercely, as the speedometer needle slipped up to seventy. "You wanna crack up and maybe conk out, so they find the gun in your pocket? You wanta ruin it all?"

He slowed down, and then he began to hear things. From the wheels, he heard things. The tires picked up some stones when he'd stopped there on the shoulder, and now the stones were talking to him.

You killed a man. You killed a man. You killed a man....

"Shut up!" Joe yelled.

He had *not* killed a man. To kill somebody, you had to hate him, didn't you? He had not hated Manning. He had not cared whether Manning lived or died. Joe was merely the means by which Manning had died. He didn't even know why Manning had to go. Manning was just a job for Joe.

"Like a steer in a packing house," Joe said. "A job."

A job for which he would receive a thousand bucks. His third job. If he hadn't tried to run up the first two thousand on Akara's roulette table, he would now have three thousand dollars. He could maybe run the third thousand up to break even. He could maybe make it five thousand, maybe ten.

He shook his head, "Lay off that stuff. Stick to business."

The business of killing.

Killed a man. Killed a man. Killed a man....

He listened for a moment, and then cursed terribly. Think of something else, Joe. Think of when you make your pile. Twenty grand, say. You go somewhere far away and forget all this. South America. Find yourself a sweet, dark-eyed kid and settle down. Buy yourself a plantation there, and hire some natives to do the work.

Joe laughed. It was a deep, chesty laugh, quite real. He could always send away the ghosts of dead men by substituting a vision of himself and some sweet little dark-eyed cutie sitting in a patio, drinking planters' punch, while beyond, as far as the eye could reach, his rolling land grew lush with rubber, cotton, or whatever the hell they grew in S.A.

"Coffee beans," he said aloud as he swung the car into the Outer Drive. "That's what they grow. Coffee beans."

The Drive climbed along the steep face of Pine Bluff. To his left the city dropped away, reeling slightly as the road curved. The winking lights shone like stars down there. He had risen above the stars and he had achieved a godlike mastery over all below.

And then, blasting the exalted illusion, the sign on Johnny The Turk's place loomed above, higher than Joe, higher even than the ragged pines that rimmed the bluffs.

AKARA's it said, diagonally across the sky in blue tubing. Then in flashing red a bit below:

Dine-Dance
Dine-Dance
Dine-Dance

"And me with my damn coffee beans!" Joe said bitterly. JOHNNY THE TURK AKARA had acquired the old Pendle Mansion on the bluff for a song, they said. Under the direction of the Turk's decorators, the Victorian grandeur of the place had taken on a tawdry glitter that appealed to Pendleville's

17

smart set. The Turk was doing all right for himself. And whoever was backing Johnny, Joe imagined, was doing all right too.

Though it was by now after one A.M. the parking lot was nearly full, and Joe had to look for a spot to park the car. He got out, slapping the pocket of his coat to make sure the gun was there. As he started toward the private entrance at the rear of the big house, a snake of lightning struck down into the town somewhere and the bluff trembled with reverberating thunder.

With his clumsy, rolling gait, he hurried to the door that opened directly into Akara's office and knocked hard on it.

"Me," he said nervously. "Joe."

An electric lock release buzzed. Joe grasped the knob, wrenched it, pushed open the door. Then he was all right. Before him, light fell warmly on paneled walls. There was the Turk—and a good stiff drink and a place to wash his hands. He entered, swaggering a little, a short, powerfully built blond man with a wide, pliant mouth and curiously soft brown eyes.

"Yeah," Joe said, and he put the gun down on the Turk's desk. "That was that."

Akara looked at him. That is, Joe was reasonably sure he was being looked at. The light against Akara's rimless glasses made his eyes look like the windows of an empty house. He was a tall man, Akara, with a wide, smooth, hairless face and a nearly hairless head. His skin was dark.

He was not necessarily a Turk—some kind of hunky, Joe thought—but everybody called him that. He wore good clothes, smoked slim, expensive cigars, and managed generally to create an impression of elegance.

Akara finally put out a smooth, yellowish hand, picked up the gun, carried it to a drawer. "Good boy, Joe," he said quietly.

"Sure," Joe admitted. "I want my grand."

"Right now," Akara said. He watched Joe move across to Akara's lavatory. Joe turned on the light in there, opened the water tap, but did not close the door. He did not like small, tight airless rooms.

"No trouble, Joe?" Akara asked.

"No," Joe said, scrubbing his hands. "He took it like a man." He laughed as he saw Akara's shoulders twist. "Inna belly," Joe added. "Also inna head. Joe-boy, he don't mess around."

Akara said nothing, and Joe wondered where the Turk had got the notion that there had been any trouble. Joe sometimes entertained the notion that Johnny Akara was stupid. Johnny was big, thrifty of motion, deliberate when he moved. Maybe that suggested stupidity.

Akara's hand moved to the switch of the intercom box on his desk. A light glowed. Akara said, "Thousand dollars, Jerry. C-notes." The light went out.

JOE CAME out of the lavatory, drying his hands on a small linen towel. "You'd better get some new rubber on that heap, Johnny."

Akara gave him a slow look. "Why?"

"Might leave tracks. I hadda park on the shoulder."

"I thought you said no trouble, Joe."

"No trouble, sure. I just said I hadda park on the shoulder. You want me to block the highway maybe?"

Akara drew his lips in over his teeth. His grunt was visible if not audible, jolting his big body in the chair. "If that's all—" he began.

"That's all," Joe said. He dropped the towel in the wastebasket, a habit he had acquired while working once in a barbershop. "A clean job, Johnny," he said emphatically. "I'd just play it safe if I was you. I'd switch the rubber."

Horrified, Manning took a faltering backward step.

Joe clenched his hands, testing for stickiness. He opened them, scowled at his palms.

"Blood, Joe?" Akara asked. He laughed softly as Joe, his mouth taut, his eyes startled, flung himself away from the desk toward the liquor cabinet. "Yah," Akara said, "you better have a drink."

Joe was drinking scotch out of a water tumbler when a knock sounded on the rear door. Akara buzzed the lock, and in came a thin dry wisp of a man wearing a green celluloid eyeshield. He brought a stack of currency to the desk and handed it to Akara. The thin man turned, coughing, and went back the way he had come.

Akara riffled the bills, handed them to Joe.

"Uh-huh." Joe counted the money, not without moving his lips. When he had finished, he folded the bills, put a heavy silver clip on them, tucked the packet away in his trouser pocket.

"If you didn't have a house brake on that wheel upstairs," he said, "I'd maybe go up there and run this up to five, maybe ten grand."

Akara shook his head slowly. "No brake, Joe."

Joe laughed, moving toward the outer door. "The hell." He put his hand on the knob, paused, looking back over a broad shoulder. "Well, any time, Johnny. Any time at all."

"Sure," Akara said. "I'll let you know." He turned his head, watching Joe. Outside thunder boomed hollowly as Joe opened the door and stepped across the sill.

Akara sat for a time without moving.

Then he turned slowly in the chair and picked up the 'phone. He dialed. While he waited he peeled cellophane from a cigar.

PRESENTLY HE said: "Hello… Sure, it's me. Joe was here just now… Good job, he says… Yes… Sure, boss… Two weeks, maybe?… No. No, we don't want to set a pattern… Maybe right away. Push it tomorrow… Hokay, boss. Sure."

He hung up. He nipped the cigar with strong white teeth, spat the tip toward the wastebasket, lighted the cigar. After a placid drag, he pushed back reluctantly and got to his feet. As he crossed the room his movements were fluid, effortless.

He pushed aside the liquor cabinet to reveal a small wall safe. He opened it and took out a briefcase, carried it to the desk. His dark, sparse eyebrows drew down in an uncertain frown.

Something was wrong—he did not know exactly what—but something. He lifted the briefcase, weighing it in his hand. His frown deepened. He put the case down again and a nameless dread added to the deliberation with which he opened the clasp. He had the uneasy notion that this was not his briefcase, that it was exactly like his but—newer? Lighter?

That, he decided, was impossible.

Hurriedly now, he opened the flap and spread the case wide.

Inside were a couple bundles of old cut-up newspapers. There was nothing else. The papers and books were gone. Everything that counted was gone.

Akara put a trembling hand into the case and fumbled around. He inverted the briefcase hastily and shook it. Nothing. It was not his briefcase. Somebody had managed a switch. Where? In the bar? The restaurant? Somewhere downtown the previous afternoon?

He crossed swiftly to the safe again, closed and locked it. He stepped to the liquor cabinet, his hands shaking. He started to push it back into place, then paused to listen to some sounds beyond his office. The orchestra had stopped playing thirty minutes ago. The kitchen clatter was faintly audible from the basement, and beyond that there came an ever-increasing rush like the approach of a fast train. Akara grunted.

"Now we got rain."

He pushed the cabinet back, went to the closet, and took out a soft tan felt hat and an expensive lightweight raincoat. He put on the hat and coat. He turned up the collar. There was a strained quality about his movements now, and as he moved to the door his footsteps were heavy. There was plenty hot stuff in that briefcase. If it fell into the wrong hands....

He went out. He stood for a moment beneath the entry light to make sure that the door was locked. Then, he turned abruptly in the direction of his parked car, to the left, he was almost certain that his elbow had brushed somebody standing close in to the wall of the building.

"Pardon—" Akara did not finish. There was nobody there. For an instant he stood in the rain, staring stupidly at the spot where he fully expected to see somebody, or something, that he had run against in his haste. He grunted. He took half a step, stopped again, his gaze on the concrete that was already glistening with rain.

There was a patch on the walk that did not glisten. Akara stared at it, unable to move. The dry spot was perhaps fourteen inches across at the widest, irregular in shape, and now rapidly disappearing as the heavy raindrops fell.

Akara put out an explorative foot, suspended it above the patch. He looked up slowly without seeing anything above that might have served as an obstacle to account for the dryness. He looked down again, the rain blurring his rimless spectacles. There was sweat on his forehead.

Like a man trying to shake himself out of a dream, Akara lifted a reassuring hand to touch his face.

"I must be going nuts," he muttered. Slowly he turned toward his car, and as he moved across the wet pavement, he could almost feel unseen eyes watching him in the dark.

CHAPTER 3
THE ZERO HOUR

IN THE afternoon *Daily World* there was a terse, unemotional story about the killing of George Manning II. The *World* also carried an editorial written by its editor, a young crusader, blaming the present "crime wave" on the current administration of Pendleville.

At 10:25 P.M. that night the city rooms of the *World* were dimly lighted, silent, occupied only by one night man. The hush was broken suddenly by the brisk *tack-tack* of slim high heels. A woman of about twenty-five, wearing a white linen suit that had somehow managed to retain its crispness, entered the city room and approached the only desk that was occupied.

She wore no hat. Her black hair was done in a short, pert bob. Her nose was small and tip-tilted, with tiny freckles that had resisted to the last—like the marines—every assault that cosmeticians could conceive.

The Kellys, she had been told by an understanding aunt, had all had freckles and they had carried them to their graves, proudly. Freckles and generous mouths and eyes that varied disconcertingly from blue to green depending on what the individual Kelly chose to wear and how the Kelly temper was behaving.

This Kelly, Doro—named after the understanding aunt— came up to the right side of the occupied desk, stopped in mid-stride, peered down into the shadows, and quickly drew her extended foot back. Her mouth formed a startled, "Oh!"

Crouching on its belly beside the desk was the blackest, biggest dog she had ever seen. There was Newfoundland in its massiveness and something about its narrow muzzle suggested wolfhound. Its eyes, yellowish in the light, appraising the girl steadily.

Doro Kelly put a hand down to the corner of the desk. "Nice doggie," she said, "I hope, I hope."

A big black brush of a tail swept the floor. The long head tipped to the left, ears alternately flattened and cocked.

"That's better," Doro said, still addressing the dog. "Do you belong to this, or this to you?"

This pointedly referred to the man who slept tipped back in his chair, his feet on the desk. He was small and thin and neat. Had there been two men in the room he would have probably been designated as "the light one," for he was very blond.

In a crowd of five, he mightn't have been noticed at all. He

25

wore glasses with heavy horn rims, and they were currently pushed up on an undistinguished forehead. His face in repose indicted a certain strength about the lean jaw which Doro Kelly had not discovered during the two months that Lee Allyn had been banging out copy for the *World*.

Doro Kelly smiled. "Wake up, boy," she said softly.

The "boy"—he must have been three or four years older than she—did not wake up. His breathing was deep, regular, and he did not snore. Doro put her purse down on the desk and her fists on her hips. Her eyes shifted from Allyn's face to a book of paper matches in the pressed glass ash tray. She picked up the matches.

"Sleepy Lee Allyn, they called him," she said, and jerked off a paper match, inserting it in Allyn's right shoe. "Until the day somebody gave him a hotfoot."

The dog got up onto its haunches, looking over the edge of the desk. It did not like what it saw.

Doro said, "Oh, go somewhere and gnaw a bone." She stepped back a pace, the second match not yet lighted. The dog had growled—a deep, rumbling growl of warning. Doro took another step backward. She ducked her head. "I'm sorry, Mr. Dog," she said meekly. "I hadn't the slightest idea the old man was stuffed with excelsior."

HER GAZE flicked back to Allyn's face. He had opened his eyes, and his mouth was open, too. The strength she had noticed in his jaw was gone. His face was only a face, and you saw six like it on every block.

He flipped his glasses back where they belonged, and through the thick lenses his pale eyes became small and sharp. He drew his right ankle along his extended left leg and removed the match from his shoe.

"You could lose a hand that way," Allyn said gravely. "Or a leg." He glanced down at her slim ankles, as if to imply that such a loss would be catastrophic indeed.

The dog moved about, and stood with its head pressed affectionately against Lee Allyn's right shoulder.

"Just what do you call it, Lee?"

"Blackie."

Her eyebrows rose. "How utterly original!" She saw his cheeks color faintly at her acid tone. "And when did you get him?" she asked quickly.

"Seven—no—eight years ago."

"When you were hunting big game in Africa, maybe?"

"When I was blind," he said, watching her face.

Her lip parted, her slender brows quirked. Five years as a newspaper reporter had left her hard, but she still had feelings. It showed in her eyes. She was wearing a double strand of turquoise beads, and tonight her eyes were turquoise. Lee Allyn watched her face.

She was beautiful, and he was in love with her, but he wished she had come in earlier, or not at all. Tonight, of all nights, she was going to complicate his already complicated existence. And she would ask questions, as an woman would. Embarrassing questions. Dangerous questions.

"Blind?" she repeated softly. "Lee, I didn't know. Totally?"

He nodded. Without taking his eyes off her face, he reached

unerringly for cigarettes that were on the typewriter stand to his left, behind him.

"For twelve years," he said, "It wasn't too bad. Dad owned a fruit store in Chicago. After Dad died, I gambled the fruit store against the possible failure of an expensive operation, and—" he smiled—"I won. My eyes aren't the best in the world—they kept me out of the war—but they seem pretty wonderful to me."

He offered her a cigarette, held his lighter for her, liking the way her cheeks hollowed as she drew on the flame.

He said, "The only time I can work up self-pity is when I stop to think that, if the operation hadn't succeeded, I'd have missed the sight of so lovely an Irish lass—"

"Colleen," Doro corrected archly. "Go 'long with your blarney."

"That," he said ruefully, "had the makings of a very pretty speech until you spoiled it with a grammatical technicality."

Allyn looked at his watch. He did it frequently, not out of habit but because he was always keenly aware of the rushing, relentless pressure of time—irretrievable seconds, minutes, hours.

It was 10:28. Blackie's growl had awakened him. He would have awakened not later than 10:30 anyway, for he had set the clock of his mind to that hour before stretching out for a nap. And tonight especially he must be awake and fully alert at midnight....

"I thought you were covering the Civic League meeting at the Community Building," he said to Doro. "They haven't adjourned yet, have they?"

He knew they hadn't. Steve Rice, publisher and editor of the *World*, had promised Allyn that the meeting would remain in session until well after midnight. That was to be the zero hour—for Lee Allyn.

Lee Allyn

It was no ordinary meeting. Cord Selmer, reformer, and president of the Civic League, had invited Steve Rice's father, Ira Rice, for a showdown debate on Pendleville's vice. Ira owned the city's leading industries and controlled the political party in power—and most of the criminal element as well. Along with George Yancy, Pendleville's police chief, he ran the city.

Selmer's chief purpose in calling the meeting had been to make an open demand on Ira Rice to clean up the town—or else. DORO KELLY'S mouth curved distastefully as she stubbed out her cigarette in the pressed-glass tray. "I got fed up and came back from the meeting, Lee. I hate to see a man crucify his own father. That's what Steve is doing, even if Cord Selmer is the one who is really talking. Ira Rice—" She extended a slim right foot, her eyes intent on the glossy toe of her shoe. "Well, he's just a fumbling old man now. Nothing else."

29

Allyn took his feet off the desk. Again he looked nervously at his watch. Time was short. He said, "Ira has to be eliminated. He and Yancy both. When they go, maybe we can weed out places like Canal Street, get rid of vermin like Stove Harvey and Pete Flosso. Harvey and Flosso have split this town like a melon. And they're devouring it between them."

He broke off, flushing. Doro's smile was a bit scornful. It was just talk coming from a man who was scarcely five feet and four inches, lightly built, weak-eyed.

He wondered if she would have smiled if Ed Cavanaugh, Pendleville's chief of detectives, had spoken to her like that. He decided, with a pang, that she would have given Cavanaugh all her rapt attention.

Blackie moved between them, facing Doro, his ears back. His tail wagged slowly back and forth across Allyn's knees.

Doro put out a hand and patted Blackie's head. Blackie sat down, rested his muzzle on her thigh. His eyes pleaded with her.

"He likes me, Lee," she said.

"Who could blame him?" he asked and drew a quick, shining glance from her. "What were they talking about at the Community Building when you left?"

Doro stopped petting the dog. She yawned delicately behind three fingers. "Murder," she said. "Three murders. Why three, the mystic number? Why not six or eight?"

"Irwin, Cordray, and Manning," Allyn said. "Last night Manning made it three."

"There's no connection," she argued. "Manning knew Cordray,

but they weren't friends. Men like Manning don't acquire friends. Neither of them knew Irwin."

"They all gambled," Allyn said.

Doro shrugged. "So what? So do you—the pinball machine in the Press Club." She jerked up her purse from the desk. She turned, started toward the door, and her handkerchief dropped to the floor. Allyn pointed lazily and addressed the dog.

"Blackie, pick up the handkerchief for the pretty angry lady. The pretty comma angry lady, that is."

Blackie caught up the handkerchief, trotted after Doro.

"Blackie, at least you are a gentleman," she said. Then, "Good boy. Thanks. Well, let go of it!"

Blackie refused to let go. Doro, exasperated, glanced across at Allyn. "Well, what do I have to do—roll over and play dead?"

Blackie had settled onto his haunches, jaws stubbornly locked on a corner of the fragile bit of cloth. Allyn got up, went over to stand beside Doro. He took hold of the handkerchief.

"Let go," he ordered quietly.

Blackie looked at him with soulful eyes, but he did not let go. Allyn turned to Doro just as she turned to him. Their glances touched. Then suddenly, unaccountably, he was kissing her, she was struggling a little, not much, then not at all.

Blackie had let go of the handkerchief. His tail thumped the floor.

"*That,*" Doro said as she broke away, her cheeks hot, her eyes shining, "was organized extortion—no less." She snatched the handkerchief from Allyn's hand, wheeled, went out, triumph striding with her long legs.

The slight blond man looked down at the black dog.

"Once in a while," he said, "you exhibit an uncanny sense of timing." He patted the dog on the head, turned, and approached the desk to answer the ringing 'phone.

It was Steve Rice, speaking from a booth in the Community Building. "Look, Lee, can't you hurry this thing up a little?" The publisher's voice was crisp and impatient.

Allyn sat down. "No. I can't hurry it up." He glanced at his watch. It was four minutes after eleven. "It'll be an hour, anyway. Try and hold them until then."

"But I don't see how—" Steve Rice began.

"Neither do I," Allyn broke in. "It isn't anything I can do. It's something that happens. It happens exactly at midnight. You can set your watch by it, but you can't change it. Maybe cosmic rays from the sun have something to do with it, I don't know. But with me, it's not an art, it's a—"

He hesitated, staring fixedly at the oddly luminous eyes of the black dog, but thinking of Doro Kelly and the warmth of her soft mouth.

Why not be frank about it?

"It's an affliction."

"All right," the publisher agreed, "I'll block any move toward adjournment. But this thing better be good." He hung up.

ALLYN LET the 'phone slip from his pale, sweating fingers. He wondered just how smart it had been to confide his secret to Steve Rice. Was there anything in Doro Kelly's intuitive dislike for Steve?

He lighted a cigarette, then held one hand up to the desk

light, fingers widely spread. For a long time he studied the natural aura of pink translucency outlining the bones of his fingers. He looked at his watch again and then at the big electric clock on the wall. The clock was seven minutes ahead of the watch.

He set the latter, and then, to make absolutely sure, he 'phoned time service. The clock was right. He depressed the switch on the 'phone stand and dialed the number of Mitch's Place, the newspapermen's hangout across the alley from the *World* building.

"Fritz Schoof, please," he said in the thin, futile sounding voice that he had cultivated until it was habitual. And while he waited, he alternately looked at the clock and at his splayed fingers against the light.

Schoof, the *World's* night man, answered.

Allyn said, "Fritz, this is Lee. I'm getting out of here at midnight. Got to go home." He laughed. "Well, yeah, something like that." A date. That was a laugh. You might as well say, A date with death. That would be closer.

"No reason to skip that last round of beers, Fritz. I'll hold the fort until midnight. But you'd better be here by then." He laughed again. "A friend? She hasn't got a friend at all—none that I know of!"

Allyn glanced at his watch again, urgently. "Sure, sure. Some time. Look, I've got to get out of here at midnight. You be here. Right? So long."

He hung up, put his cigarette to his mouth, and left it there. He stood up, squinting against the smoke, looked down at the black dog.

"Worried, boy?" he asked. He forced a laugh. "That makes two of us."

He crossed the city room to the door with STEVEN RICE, PUBLISHER, lettered on its frosted glass. He took keys from the pocket of his seersucker trousers, unlocked the door, went in, and waited for the black dog to follow.

He closed the door, walked unhesitantly through the gloom of the outer office into the total dark of the room beyond. He coughed, and the sound bounced. He located the desk, then the lamp, which he turned on.

The room was paneled in chestnut, the blind of the single window closed. Allyn opened the door of a closet, and on the inner side of the door there was a full length mirror.

Allyn took out a wire coat hanger which he put down on the seat of a chair. Turning toward the desk, he removed a cylindrical bottle from the pocket of his seersucker suit coat. It contained a mild saline solution and two concave pieces of optical glass. Contact lenses.

Allyn took off his horn-rimmed spectacles, folded them, put them into his pocket. The big dog whimpered, and Allyn shook his head.

"You're not going anywhere, Blackie. Not tonight."

The dog sighed and crouched, long head between forepaws, eyes watching the man. Allyn sat down behind Rice's desk, and put the contact lenses in his eyes.

It was now 11:28 by his watch.

ALLYN DUG into the pockets of his suit coat again, brought out a flat paper bag. He removed his suit coat and flung it onto the nearby chair. His tie and shirt followed. Beneath he wore a white T-shirt of elastic knit, fine gauge woolen yarn that fitted him like a second skin. He was surprisingly well-muscled.

He took off his shoes and socks. The paper bag contained white socks of the same light grade wool, and to these he had attached soles of thin, tough rawhide stitched to the wool by means of transparent gut thread. He put these on. Standing, he removed the trousers of his suit. Beneath he wore tight trunks of the same white wool.

He lighted another cigarette from the butt of the one smoldering in the tray. He mightn't have another chance to smoke before dawn. Glass bottle, suction cup, paper bag, and finally his watch went into the pockets of his suit coat. Then he hung his clothes on the hanger, stepped to the black dog. Blackie looked up, head cocked.

Allyn said, "I don't blame you. What the well-dressed man will underwear." He shook the clothes on the hanger in front of the dog's muzzle. "Watch, Blackie."

The dog got up onto its haunches, watched expectantly while Allyn carried the clothes to Steve Rice's closet and hung them up. Blackie moved over to the closet door.

"Nobody—but nobody, understand?" Allyn said. Then he stepped back to the chair behind Rice's desk and sat down. He leaned back, drew on his cigarette, and forced himself to relax. From here on out, he could only guess at time, or snatch a glance at clocks or watches other than his own.

Every now and then he would raise a hand against the rays

from the desk lamp and stare at it. No change, and there would be no change until five or six minutes before midnight.

And then it began to happen.

He noticed it first at his fingertips when he brought them up against the light. It always began there. The pink of the natural aura became less pink, gradually fading until the dark shadows that were finger bones became as distinct as though he had placed his hand above a fluoroscope. Next, the shadows would thin and then fade utterly....

Allyn stood up. He stepped in front of the mirror on the open closet door to watch the process which he had watched at every midnight during the past three and one half months. As often as he had seen it, it still held a strange, terrible fascination for him.

The big dog at his feet became attentive, sniffing the air, worriedly, whimpering.

"It's all right, boy," Allyn said softly to him.

Swiftly, now, his undistinguished face became the merest shade of itself, the bones of the skull clearly defined at first, then fading to light gray, blurring out of the picture. The gray mass that was his brain blurred out of the picture, too, and now above the shoulders of the T-shirt, the slats of the Venetian blind behind him extended in unbroken lines across the reflective surface of the mirror.

Arms and their bones had already dissolved to complete transparency, the legs also. And now a pair of trunks and T-shirt, seemingly suspended in midair and faintly luminous, melted entirely from view as the invisible rays that emanated from his body flowed through each cell of the animal fibers.

Footprints in the long-napped carpet indicated where he stood. Two pin-pricks of reflected light on the contact lens marked the location of his eyes. But Allyn himself had become as nothing, a visual cipher.

A zero.

CHAPTER 4
"I CAN USE YOU!"

THE FIRST time it had happened, he had almost lost his mind.

He would always remember that unseasonably warm night in spring, when he had slept fitfully in his stuffy little room at the Lockridge Research Foundation near Chicago. His eye operation had given him vision that was vastly better than the darkness to which he had become accustomed, but it did not measure up to standards set by every branch of the armed services. In an effort to contribute something to the war effort he had offered himself as a human guinea pig for the purposes of medical research.

There had been many tests. Even now he did not know which of the radioactive substances that had been employed, or what combination of them, had been responsible for the phenomenon. The last experiment to which he had been subjected had amounted to what Dr. Lockridge himself had said was "a terrific jolt of radioactive arsenic." It had been thought to offer a curative key to the baffling puzzles of leukemia and Hodgkin's disease.

That warm and breathless night he had awakened before

dawn. Unable to get back to sleep, or to find a cool spot on the bed, even after he had shed his pajamas, he had finally got up for a drink from the faucet above the tiny lavatory in the corner of his room. He had not turned on the light; his years of blindness had made it unnecessary. His hand went out and closed on the empty glass. Cold moonlight slanted through the window, and he saw the glass.

He did not see his hand.

He had felt the tight gathering of his frown. He clutched the glass, felt its thick hard substance, felt pain of exertion in fingers, palm, knuckles.

But where was his hand?

He had fumbled upward for the light above the mirror, the wild thought assailing him that some new form of ocular defect was responsible. The light came on, flooding the room with brilliance, dazing him. There was the mirror, and it held within its silvery pool the picture of the room and all its furnishings—Lee Allyn's room in the Lockridge Research Foundation building.

But where was Lee Allyn?

He saw the drinking glass suspended in midair above the lavatory, its edges blurred in his defective vision. He saw the glass and dropped it, saw it shatter against the basin. Then, reeling under the impact of what he saw, or failed to see, he fell and struck the floor. He knew the pain and heard all the sound that accompanied his fall.

My God, what's happened to me?

He had crawled, then, to the little table where he had laid his glasses. He put them on, his unseen hands feeling the shape of his invisible face. He stood waveringly, and in the mirror he saw a pair of horn-rimmed glasses, floating in the air. The room, the furniture, all showed in sharper focus, everything exactly placed.

Everything except Lee Allyn....

And then, at dawn, after a sleepless, wild night of hell and terror, he had watched himself gain visual substance until his naked body was as opaque as any other naked body.

THE DOCTORS had made their tests. They asked him questions, none of which were, "Did you disappear last night— that is, become so completely transparent as to be invisible?" They had not, then, expected any such miracle to happen.

Perhaps it hadn't actually happened, anyway, and if it hadn't, he certainly wasn't going to tell them he thought it had. He wasn't going to have them think him mad.

The night that followed he did not go to bed but sat, dressed in his pajamas, in the chair beside the window. The fear that it might happen again was strong, but stronger still was the fear that it had never really happened at all. That he was mad.

At midnight it recurred, the whole process occupying not more than six minutes of time. And then his mirror showed him a pair of cotton pajamas well filled, with his invisible substance striding anxiously up and down.

He felt perfectly normal. His senses were unimpaired. He sat down again to consider the whole fantastic situation carefully. He concluded that the thing to do was to tell Dr. Lockridge.

He got up, went to the closet, and began to pull on a pair of wool trousers. It was then that he noticed something else unbelievably odd.

Where the wool cloth pressed tightly against his body, it too became translucent at first, and then wholly transparent.

"I'm a damned X-ray machine!" he muttered.

He kicked off the trousers and dropped once more into the chair to try and think things through. Whatever the nature of the rays that emanated from his body, they were selective. The cotton of his pajamas was not affected, but wool, an animal fiber, was. If he wanted to be seen, he could put on clothing of linen or cloth, shoes of rubber and canvas, some sort of a mask.

When the phenomenon occurred again and again with clock-work regularity, Allyn began to condition his just-average brain to accept it.

He was quite sure he would not like to be exhibited as a freak. A retiring young man to begin with, capable of self-effacement, he had no desire to see his name in print in Ripley's column. Nor did the idea that he might become a ward of the state—a national curiosity—appeal to him.

In the end, he decided that destiny must govern the matter. He would neither reveal nor conceal his affliction—if that was what it was—and if the doctors did not discover it for themselves, he would not tell them.

They had not discovered it, and he had not told them.

Until he had come to Pendleville and approached the *World's* Steve Rice, Lee Allyn's applications for work had met cold refusals. Steve Rice had given him a break, probably, because the *World* was understaffed and had trouble holding employees, due to tough competition from the *Sentinel*.

During the three months which he had served on the *World*,

Allyn had devoted more time and effort to the study of Pendleville's internal conditions than he had to his actual assignments. Pendleville, he discovered, was an Augean stable overdue for a cleaning—and Ira Rice was the stable-master.

Allyn had observed Steve Rice, Ira's son, carefully, in the three month period. Nothing that Steve had done seemed to indicate that he was other than a selfish and earnest man devoted to righting the wrongs of his father.

The night before Manning's murder, Allyn had taken Steve Rice into his confidence, demonstrating his invisibility.

"It's a trick," Steve Rice had told the invisible presence, "but it's a damned good trick. I can use you, Allyn, in my clean-up campaign. You'll be my captain." He'd laughed. "Captain Zero. How's that for a name for a nothingness?"

Allyn wondered now if he should have told Steve Rice his secret. He had not liked Steve's words: "I can use you." He had eventually decided to go along with the publisher anyway, realizing that Steve Rice was probably more intelligent than he himself was....

ALLYN CLOSED the door of the closet in Steve Rice's office. Blackie pushed up onto his haunches, thumped the floor with his tail, and stared at the spot where he knew his invisible master was standing. The dog looked eager and expectant.

Allyn said, "Nothing doing, boy. You've got your job, and I've got mine. Yours is to watch those clothes. Don't let anybody come in here, get it? Watch, boy. Watch."

Allyn turned out the desk light, moved through the darkness to the door. Blackie whimpered.

"Watch," Allyn repeated. "Nobody—but nobody—gets in here." He went out, passed by the desk of Steve Rice's secretary, and out into the big gloomy city room. Fritz Schoof, the night man, reeking of beer, came swaying through the door at the top of the broad stairs.

Allyn stopped, his back against a glass partition, and waited until Schoof was halfway across the city room before he went through the door.

Then he went down the short flight of stairs and out onto the sidewalk. At the corner of Main and Washington, he waited, like any other careful citizen, for the green light to halt the stream of cars. Being unseen, he was in great danger of becoming a traffic casualty.

Across the street, City Park with its ancient elms arching high above the well-kept lawn, presented a clear field. He ran toward the Community Building, a native sandstone structure in the Colonial manner, situated at the north end.

To Lee Allyn, just an average guy, a door was just a door. Captain Zero, his alter ego, was forced to be more specific about doors—to classify them. There were doors that were headaches and doors that were half-headaches: the former being largely or entirely of transparent glass; the latter having a clear glass insert.

Then there were doors which he liked to refer to as "lead pipe cinches." The door of the Community Building fell into the lead pipe class, being tall and massive and thoroughly opaque. Such a door he would open only a little way, far enough to sidle through, and immediately let it fall back into place. If this was seen from the inside, anyone would obviously conclude that somebody had changed his mind about entering.

Zero slipped into a deserted foyer—softly carpeted, dammit! he observed, thus capable of revealing every step he took. Beyond that he could see the small auditorium and a group of forty people that Steve Rice and Cord Selmer had brought together to discuss the city's crime problem. And, incidentally, to hear an indictment of Ira Rice's hand-picked administration.

Cord Selmer, a thin man with quick gray eyes, was seated on the stage nibbling a thumbnail, and there were others. Zero did not linger but turned to the left along the foyer to enter one of the anterooms.

AS THE door opened, Steve Rice, who was there by previous arrangement, got up from a club chair. He was somewhat above medium height, middle-aged, solidly packed into conservative gray gabardine. His high forehead sloped to a receding line of fine, kinky, black hair. His eyes were brown and blunt.

"I can hear you breathe," he said critically.

"Good Lord," Allyn said in the voice of Zero, *"you didn't expect me to give that up, did you?"*

"Are you all set?"

Zero laughed nervously. *"I've got the shakes."*

"Nobody's going to notice it."

"I've never made a speech. What'll I say, Steve?"

Rice lighted a cigarette. "Weren't you out scouting around last night? Didn't you pick up anything?"

"A kick into a gulley," Zero said. *"I picked that up when I tried to follow Manning into that wildcat hack. I made a mistake calling*

43

him up and speaking to him maybe, but I wanted to warn him."

"Warn him?" Steve Rice frowned. "You mean you knew ahead of time that Manning was going to be killed?"

"It was a hunch. He seemed to fit the same gambler's pattern as Irwin and Cordray. He was alone and vulnerable. After I lost Manning I went out to that new gambling place on the Bluff—Johnny Akara's."

"And you didn't pick up anything you might throw at the Old Man tonight?"

Doro Kelly

"No. I got rained out."

Steve Rice's eyes were shrewd. "You can't operate in the rain, huh?"

"I can," Zero said stiffly. *"I prefer not to."* Rain deflected by his substance could locate him exactly, especially if he happened to pass through a beam of light. He watched Steve Rice toying with a thin gold lighter.

"I've got something," the publisher said, "if I knew exactly what it was and how to use it."

"Maybe," Zero suggested, *"if you'd tell me what it is...."*

But Rice was shaking his head, his lips tightly compressed.

"You've got a cute trick there. But if you don't mind, Captain, I'll handle the strategy. Now go on in and throw the fear of God into them. We've as much as told Yancy what we think of his law enforcement. My Old Man has risen to Yancy's defense. Go on in and heckle him. Bluff him out."

Steve Rice broke off. The door of the anteroom had opened and closed. He took an uncertain step toward it, dark eyes darting about.

"Zero!" he snapped.

There was no answer.

Rice stood there, nervously licking his lips. "Damn that guy," he muttered. "I hope I haven't made a mistake."

CHAPTER 5
UNKNOWN VOYAGER

O N THE left side aisle, four rows from the front and somewhat apart from the group of indignant citizens which comprised the Civic League—George Yancy, Pendleville's chief of police, sprawled in his seat. He was a big man, gone to paunch, slovenly. His uniform, freshly pressed for this evening, hung about him in tired lines. He used his vizored cap as a fan to stir a breeze against his perspiring red face.

Cord Selmer was, in Yancy's opinion, a pipsqueak. Selmer's Civic League was a storm in a water glass. Yancy was not worried. Old Ira would take care of him. Old Ira damned well had to, with all that Yancy had on Ira.

Right now, up there on the stage, old Ira was telling the group about the accomplishments of the old current administration. Pointing with Pride. If Yancy knew old Ira, Ira could Point with Pride louder and longer even than Cord Selmer could View with Alarm.

Yancy snorted. Look at the turnout Selmer had got tonight, he thought contemptuously. Just a handful. Yancy's piggy eyes darted about, picking faces out of the crowd. They touched Steve Rice.

They moved on to a girl with dark hair who was currently patting away a yawn, and there they lingered only because the girl was a damned good looker. Doro Kelly, wasn't that her name? She worked on the *World*. Yancy momentarily allowed himself to think of Mrs. Yancy, who would be snoring in bed with her hair done up in enough hardware to sink a battleship.

He sighed, and his gaze flipped to the face next to Doro's and a good foot above. There it stopped.

Yancy thought, What the hell are you doing here?

The face next to Doro's was dark and homely and it gave the impression of being carved out of hard wood. It suggested vigor and indomitable purpose. Its eyes could measure you, weigh you, cast you aside. Yancy did not like the face because the eyes *had* measured and weighed him, and they had found him wanting.

Yancy often wondered exactly what he was going to do with Ed Cavanaugh. He knew now what he should not have done. He should not have kicked Cavanaugh upstairs to the detective bureau. He ought to have framed Cavanaugh and gotten rid of him.

Yancy's attention shifted to the rugged old man with the silvery mane who was haranguing the group from the speaker's rostrum.

"You tell 'em, Ira," Yancy mentally cheered.

"... And let me assure you, my good friends and neighbors," Ira Rice was saying, "that here in Pendleville we have the lowest statistical record of unsolved homicides of any industrial city in these United States!"

"It's a pretty low record, all right."

The voice was resonant, carrying. Its inflections etched the statement with acid. It came from above and somewhat in front of Yancy, and it momentarily disconcerted the hardened old campaigner.

47

Ira Rice's eyes lifted to the box nearest the stage on the left side. Yancy, by craning his neck, could see three spindly chairs, empty as were all the chairs in the other boxes on both sides of the auditorium. He was aware that others were looking in the same direction.

Ira Rice took out a breast pocket handkerchief and wiped his great lump of a nose. He took a deep breath, opened his mouth. But before he could say anything, the voice from the box came again:

"Only three unsolved homicides at the present time. Count them. Irwin, Cordray, and Manning."

There was a ripple of excitement across the crowd and then a listening hush as the voice went on.

"And speaking of statistics, Mr. Rice, you might point out that we have, in Pendleville, an unequaled record for extending paid protection to organised vice."

"Sa—ay—" Yancy wallowed up out of his seat to stand in the aisle. There he hesitated, watching Ira Rice as the latter moved away from the rostrum and to the left side of the stage. There he stood, eyes elevated.

"Sir," Ira said with dignity, "when you address me, will you be courteous enough to show your face?"

"You're looking at it," the voice retorted. *"I can't help it if you can't see me. Maybe it's your astigmatism. Maybe that's what keeps you from seeing that string of dives Pete Flosso operates on Canal Street. Maybe that's why you can't see Stove Harvey's Little Casino, his Palermo Club, and half a dozen other joints that add to the spotless reputation of our city!*

"Or maybe you're wearing Yancy's blinders—you know, the gold-plated ones bought with pay-off money from boys like Harvey, Flosso, and Johnny Akara."

"That's enough of that!" Yancy growled. "They've rigged up some of a gadget, Ira. Some loudspeaker business up there. There isn't one among 'em man enough to say those things to your face."

"I resent that, Yancy," the voice went on, unperturbed. *"I resent being called a gadget. I'm no gadget. I'm a phenomenon."*

Yancy, purpling with rage, stumbled across the aisle to the arched opening and onto the flight of stairs leading to the box.

"I intend to prove every charge against the Ira Rice machine, made or implied here tonight. I intend to show you every human rat that runs in the sewers of his community, so you can drive them out into the open where the decent can pass judgment upon them. I will prove—"

Yancy's thick arm swept aside the rose velvet that draped the entrance to the box, and the voice broke off. Yancy looked down at the stage, at old Ira, and grinned. His vicious little eyes swept along the floor, along the rail. Then he stepped forward, turned completely around, and stared at the wall.

In the auditorium there was utter silence with every eye focused on the box where Yancy stood.

"WHAT—NO GADGETS, *Yancy? No loudspeaker? Not even a lonely little radio tube?"*

The voice. The damned mocking voice! Yancy turned swiftly. Somebody laughed—but not Yancy. His gold-braided cap was lifted from the top of his head, whirled out over the auditorium.

49

The rose curtain bellied out. Yancy lunged heavily, both arms wide, snatched and held the curtain, released it a fold at a time, his eyes refusing to believe its emptiness.

The crowd roared. Doro Kelly turned shining eyes on Ed Cavanaugh's wooden-Indian profile.

"Ed, what is it? Who's up there in the box with Yancy?"

Cavanaugh had no answer. Cord Selmer was rapping his gavel for silence. On the stage beside him stood Steve Rice, a grim smile on his lips.

"Fellow citizens, quiet," Selmer urged. "Please. My friend Steve Rice has a word of explanation."

A chorus of *sh's* arose from the audience as Steve Rice took Selmer's place behind the rostrum.

"Friends," Steve began, "I merely want to assure you that Captain Zero is not a gadget. Not a thing of wires and radio tubes. Captain Zero is a man. A living, breathing man, and he may be down there among you right now."

There were uneasy murmurings. Steve went on.

"I have talked with Captain Zero in my apartment. I have talked to him without seeing him. I have felt his hand grasp mine, without actually seeing his hand. How he accomplishes this feat of invisibility. I do not know, and if I did I would not tell you.

"All I know of Captain Zero is that he is working for the good of the community, that his enemies are those who betray public trust for personal gain. You will hear much more of Captain Zero."

Zero heard Steve Rice's confident words from the foyer of the

Community Building. He turned now from the open door of the auditorium. He stopped literally in his tracks—his betraying tracks in the soft carpet.

Chief Yancy was standing between Zero and the massive front door. Yancy's sharp little eyes were on the carpet, his big red fists clenched.

"Step aside, Yancy," Zero warned softly. *"You heard what the man said about people who betray public trust for personal gain."*

Yancy didn't say anything. He watched the tracks advance a step nearer. He stood his ground.

"Maybe I'm under arrest," Zero said mockingly. *"Is that it? What's the charge—telling the truth?"*

"You keep your distance, damn you!" As Yancy went for his gun, Zero sprang, not straight at the chief but to the right. Yancy, using his gun like a hatchet, hacked at thin air. The spent force of the blow carried him forward and off balance, with most of his weight on his left leg. Zero's foot shot out in front of Yancy's left ankle, and it took only a slight push to spill the police chief onto the floor.

Zero brushed through the door, rounded the building to enter a parking lot. He spotted Ira Rice's black Packard, and headed toward it, walking carefully across the white crushed stone.

Transportation, he reflected, was going to be a hell of a problem during the hours between midnight and dawn. He couldn't drive—for how far would an apparently driverless car go before every motor cop on duty was howling at his heels? And if you were not seen, exactly how did you go about flagging a cab? As to bus and trolley facilities, there was nothing of the kind after 2 A.M.

I need help, he thought. Somebody with faith in me. I don't think that somebody is Steve Rice.

He thought of Doro Kelly. He tried to picture himself going up to Doro and saying, "Look, Miss Kelly, you can't see me, but I'd like to hitch a ride." At which point Doro would either faint, or scream for help.

IT WAS no less awkward when he came up to Ira Rice's Packard and saw a man in chauffeur's garb slumped behind the wheel.

He glanced about warily. Then he stepped boldly to the left front door of the Packard and jerked it open. Ira's sleeping chauffeur fell against Zero's chest. He got out one startled bleat, coming awake, and then Zero's left arm looped about his throat and tightened.

The chauffeur clawed at the invisible thing which was stifling him. Zero's right hand moved across the man's chest, under the whipcord jacket, and pulled the chauffeur's under-arm gun. He slammed the barrel of the automatic across the side of the man's head. The chauffeur slumped.

He dropped the gun on the seat cushions, shoved the unconscious man back into the seat, closed the car door and leaned back against it.

Two men came directly toward the Packard, and Zero recognized the voices of Cord Selmer and Steve Rice.

"I've got a bottle in the car," Steve said.

"I don't ordinarily indulge, but this is a special occasion. A very special occasion." Selmer slapped the younger man across the shoulders. "Honestly, I'll never forget Yancy's face."

"Nor the Old Man's," Steve said. "We've got him on the defensive, Cord, for the first time in years."

"How does he do it—that Zero friend of yours?" Selmer wanted to know.

They were within two feet of "that Zero friend" who had given up breathing, whose trembling brought tiny creaking sounds from the car against which he'd flattened himself. They veered away, Steve Rice and Selmer. Thank God they veered. When they rounded the Packard, approaching the car next to it, Steve said with assurance:

"It's some sort of a trick. Wasn't it Robert-Houdin, the magician, who claimed he could make the whole of the French army invisible if they'd pay him enough?"

"But who is Zero, actually?"

For a moment, Steve Rice was silent. Zero listened intently, wondering if Steve would break his pledge of secrecy, naming himself several kinds of a fool for ever having confided in Steve.

"That's something I can't tell you, Cord."

Zero took a deep breath.

"You'd rather not?" Selmer persisted. "Or don't you know?"

"I do not know," Steve lied.

The two men got into Steve Rice's car. It backed around and headed into the street. Zero turned around, opened the door of the Packard, caught the unconscious chauffeur under the arms, dragged him out and into the thick shrubbery nearby.

He stripped off the chauffeur's light jacket and pants and

put these on. A scrap of cloth ripped from the man's shirt served as a crude mask for Zero's unseen face. He added the vizored cap which, like the pants and jacket, was several sizes too large for him. He went back to the Packard, a dusky figure in the uncertain light.

Ira Rice

He had just assumed the position in which he had found the chauffeur when Ira Rice himself came stumping across the crushed stone and toward the car, alone and muttering angrily.

"…Man you can't see! Rubbish! Invisible investigator, my left leg! Some scurvy trick of that whelp of mine. Damned childish trick!" Now abreast of the car, Ira bellowed, "Jordan, what the hell kind of a bodyguard are you, asleep at the switch again!" He jerked the car door open.

Zero's right hand scooped up the chauffeur's gun. He turned out of the car, facing Ira, and shoved the automatic into Ira's middle.

"Not a squeak," he warned, the steadiness of his eerie voice incongruous with his inner trembling.

"You!" Ira gasped recognizing the voice that had heckled him in the auditorium. "I *knew* it was some kind of a scurvy trick with wires and—and some kind of gadget. Why, you little, insignificant—" He raised a clenched fist that trembled. He grunted as the gun drove deeper into his belly.

"You're going to get in and drive."

"I'll be damned if—"

"You'll be damned if you don't." Zero took a sidling step that allowed Ira to reach position under the wheel. Ira, spluttering helpless protests, got in under the wheel. Zero opened the rear door, ducked in, letting Ira feel the cold muzzle of the gun at the back of the neck. Ira shuddered and moved.

"All the way out to that castle of yours, I'll be watching you. We're going to have a talk, Ira. Just you and I."

And Zero settled back, assuming the attitude of a man lounging on a powder keg.

CHAPTER 6
TRACK OF THE KILLER

T HE HOUSE on Northern Heights Road was—like Ira Rice himself—substantial though old. It was constructed of rough-hewn stone. There were some who thought it had the aspects of a jail. That was appropriate enough—or would have been, had there been any means of keeping Ira confined to it.

The old man slewed the big car into the winding drive beneath the massive oaks, and stopped with a scuffing of rubber and gravel before the front door.

"Now what do you want me to do?" he asked gamely. "Crawl up the steps backwards on my hands and knees?"

There was no answer.

Ira turned as far in the seat as he could. He blinked.

"Bah!" he said. "Trying to frighten an old man! Idiots!" He scrambled about, rammed at the door latch with the heel of his hand, paused with one foot out of the car.

Just exactly how had the stranger gotten out of his car? At the boulevard stop? Why hadn't he heard the door open?

For a moment he considered getting a jackhandle out of the trunk and using it to beat about in the rear compartment of the car.

"I'm damned if I will," he said, and got out. "I'm damned if I'll start looking under the bed at my age!"

He pounded up the stone steps to the front door, where he used his latchkey. He entered the hall, turned into the library where a brass lamp with a green glass shade burned on a table of carved walnut. He took off his hat, tossed it into a chair. He put up his thick gnarled hands and rumpled his shock of silvery hair.

His thin-lipped mouth twitched as he took up a decanter from the tray on the table, pouring brandy liberally, regretting that, in the agitation, he had slopped some of it.

There had been a time in his early life when he thought that if he could ever reach the point where he could afford to have brandy and a good cigar after dinner, he would be content. It was that small ambition from which the larger ones had grown, so that he sometimes thought of his empire as having been built on brandy.

56

It was in the pre-brandy stage that he had gotten hold of the Selmer Drop-Forge Company, then a tottering industry controlled by Cord Selmer's uncle, an old man, too sick mentally to know what he was signing and too close to the grave to care.

The business had mushroomed under Ira Rice's vigorous ruthless cultivation. Ira had built a foundry, had bought a brick kiln, and a chain of hardware stores to market tools of his own manufacture. Into every fire old Ira thrust an iron until more than half of the families in the rapidly growing city depended upon his fortune for their own.

He owned a controlling interest in Pendleville, financially and politically. It was an empire that would, he had vowed, last as long as he lasted, despite the internal rumblings he heard and shut his ears against. In spite of the rat-gnawings of an ungrateful son who hated him and all he represented, it would last a long time.

Ira tasted the brandy. He said, "Ah!" in appreciation, put the glass down, and started around the table toward the 'phone. He'd call George Yancy, he thought, and put the police on the lookout for that fool chauffeur. How to describe the man with the mask? Well, he was short and he wore a mask. He also wore a chauffeur's whipcord uniform three sizes too large for him. It wasn't much, but it was more than "a man you couldn't see."

Ira put a hand out toward the 'phone.

"Don't do that, Ira."

THE VOICE again. Ira whipped around, his dark eyes protruding from their leathery lids. He turned slowly, fastened his gaze on the small radio built into the bookcase.

"No, no, Ira," the voice said from the opposite side of the room.

Ira faced the voice. There was a chair with down-filled cushions in the corner. He saw, to his horror, that the seat of the chair was depressed under the weight of an invisible presence.

He said, "Dammit, I don't believe in you!"

"Please don't bother to try," the voice said mildly, "if it's too much of a strain. And you'd better sit down. You look like you might have a stroke. You can't imagine how difficult it would be for me to have to go for a doctor. So difficult that I mightn't bother."

Ira groped behind him, backed up until he found a chair, and sat down on the edge of it. "I still don't believe in you, understand?" he growled. "I've been consuming just a little too much brandy lately—that's the trouble." He watched the upholstery on the back of the chair opposite. Captain Zero leaned back. Ira shook himself.

"How the hell did you get in here?" he bellowed.

"Walked in right behind you. Incidentally, you'll find your chauffeur's uniform somewhere between Mason and Elm Streets. I shoved the clothes out the window of the car as we rode along. It seemed the best way."

Ira dashed a hand through his hair. "Well, what do you want?" she asked.

"A lot," the voice said flatly. "First, I want to know about Irwin, Cordray, and Manning. Why were they killed?"

"How would I know?" the old man snarled.

"This is your town, isn't it?" The voice was faintly mocking. "Don't you know what goes on in your own back yard?"

"No, dammit!" Ira pounded the chair arm. "I can't be expected to know everything!"

"But you do know where Pete Flosso and Stove Harvey came from. And who brought them here. Who was it?"

Ira scowled silently at the chair across the room.

The voice went on. *"Flosso and Harvey came here from Chicago at the head of a squad of goons. You were having labor trouble and you needed some strong-arm organisers to get things under control again.*

"Flosso and Harvey liked the set-up and decided to stay. They liked the idea of a mayor who was your yes-man, and a council that they had helped put into office. They liked the idea of a police chief who could be handled.

"No, Ira, it isn't your town any more. It belongs to Pete Flosso and Stove Harvey, and they've split it between them. And you—oh, it's okay for you to sit in the driver's seat with the broken reins in your hands. You make a nice target for all that heat that Cord Selmer and your son Steve can turn on you."

The old man grunted.

"Things," he admitted, "have gotten a little out of hand. That happens. A machine gets too big for a man to handle." He moved to the desk, picking up the glass of brandy in his left hand, shifted it around behind the table, right hand dangling. He sipped a little brandy.

"I've sometimes thought that if we got rid of George Yancy, put this man Cavanaugh in his place—"

It was something he had never seriously considered, he had

not dared to consider for fear of recriminations. Cavanaugh might have the guts to clean house....

IRA WAS now in front of a shallow drawer in the table—a drawer which was visible from the chair Zero sat in. Ira raised his glass again. His right hand pulled the drawer open. Reflected in the curved sides of the brandy glass he could see the glint of the small automatic in the drawer. He lowered the glass, his eyes following it and then jumping to the gun.

The gun seemed to have come to life. It tipped up in the drawer, butt first, lifted into the air, its muzzle describing an arc that stopped directly over Ira's heart.

"Maybe you've never noticed," Zero said, *"but down-filled cushions retain their impression for quite a while. And another thing, Ira, every time I see a right-handed man start hoisting his brandy sniffer in his left hand, I begin to worry about what the hell he intends to do with that right hand."*

Ira, his mouth still open, his throat dry, saw the automatic float back from him. And he saw something else—two pinpoints of greenish light originating at the desk lamp and reflected in the eyes of Captain Zero.

The old man said haltingly, "I—I guess you're the real McCoy."

"Thanks," Zero said dryly.

Ira moved around the table, sank down slowly on the arm of his chair. The automatic had come to rest on the end table beside the down-filled chair. It was not pointing at him. It didn't have to point at him. He knew he was licked. His fingers drummed uneasily on his thighs. He pushed his lips into a friendly smile.

"Yes, the real McCoy," he repeated. "Captain Zero, how would you like to work for me?"

Zero laughed. *"Are you kidding?"*

"No, indeed, I'm not. I think you can clean up this town."

"I think I can, too."

"I can't be of much help to you," Ira went on, "for as I said, things have gotten a little out of hand. But I can tell you where to start. There's a girl by the name of Ivy Lindhorst. Girl, hell—she's a woman and a beautiful one. A mercenary baggage, understand—don't trust her—but she's known a lot of men who've come up from nothing in the past ten years. Flosso, Harvey, Johnny The Turk—she knows them all. You might be able to beg, buy, or steal some dirt about them from her."

Zero laughed gently. *"Ivy Lindhorst. Fair enough. I'll start with her. And from her—"*

Zero broke off as the 'phone on the carved walnut table rang. Old Ira put out a hand, paused, glancing toward the spot where he presumed Zero to be.

"May I?" he asked timidly.

"Why not? You pay the bill, don't you?"

Ira picked up the handset and growled hello. On the other end of the line a voice that was unpleasantly matter-of-fact said, "Ed Cavanaugh. Detective Bureau. Sorry to have to tell you this, Mr. Rice, but something has happened to your son."

"To—" The old man swallowed past the dryness in his throat. He clutched the edge of the table.

"He was found on the sidewalk in front of his apartment

building," Cavanaugh went on. "He was dead. Looks like he'd fallen from the penthouse. And I don't think he jumped."

Ira lowered the receiver slowly, pressed it into its cradle. He kept right on pressing it, pushing down on the 'phone as if by sheer force he could smash the thing and its terrible capacity for carrying bad news. His mouth worked spasmodically before any words would come.

"Steve—my boy—dead. Murdered. They murdered my boy." His big face crumpled.

Zero said, *"That makes four."*

CHAPTER 7
DEATH FROM NOWHERE

FOUR BLOCKS from the business district but definitely on the right side of Main Street were the Shelton Arms Apartments. There were three buildings, two low and out-flung from a big tower of smooth yellow brick. The tower rose twelve stories above a formal sunken garden.

The body of Steve Rice had been removed, but the spot where it had landed—the wide brick patio between entryway and garden—was marked by a small but excited group of tenants in various stages of dress and undress.

All eyes were turned toward the driveway. The right front door of a big Packard swung open. Ira Rice squirmed across the seat and got out, his movements labored. He gave the door a half-hearted push that failed to close it. The door yawned open again as Ira plodded up the brick paved walk.

Zero, who had ridden in the back seat of the Packard, scrambled out, took quick silent strides that brought him directly behind Ira as the latter approached the group in front of the entryway.

A man sitting on the stone bench said, "Hello, Mr. Rice."

Ira didn't say anything. His face was stony, his eyes bleak. He stepped to the door, where he was met by a uniformed cop.

"Where's my boy?" he asked hoarsely.

The officer, a young man with a smooth, pink-cheeked face, shook his head. "Mr. Rice, he—uh, the other Mr. Rice he went—that is, they took him—" He swallowed, tried again. "He was dead, see, and Cavanaugh—"

Ira turned, started back the way he had come. The young cop put out a hand, caught Ira's sleeve.

"Cavanaugh wants to talk to you, Mr. Rice."

Ira, his teeth clenched, turned, shaking a gnarled fist in the young officer's face. "No!" he shouted. "I'm going to my son. Tell Cavanaugh unless he finds my boy's killer in twenty-four hours, I'll break him. Break him—have you got that in your stupid head?"

The cop gulped and nodded. He stood for a moment watching the broken old man stumble off toward the Packard, then turned back into the house and went toward the elevator.

Zero was close behind the policeman.

The man in the elevator wore blue coveralls, smoked a corn cob pipe, and his glasses were mended with adhesive tape. A janitor, probably.

"Kind of got yourself told off, didn't you, copper?" he cackled. He jerked the elevator door shut, missing Zero's heel. The policeman had moved into one corner of the car and stood with arms folded, face flushed, eyes sullen.

Zero took the opposite corner, watched the indicator. The elevator door opened, and Zero followed the cop out into a small square hall. Half a dozen reporters representing both the *Sentinel* and the *World* were hanging around the door of Steve Rice's apartment, their entrance barred by a flashy and perspiring policeman.

The young cop pushed on through to the door. Zero, scarcely daring to breath, came immediately behind him.

"Where's the Old Man, Jim?" the fat cop asked.

The other shook his head. "Mr. Rice went off to the morgue. I gotta see Cavanaugh." He opened the door, paused as Jeff Binkley of the *Sentinel* called after him:

"While you're at it, tell Cavanaugh to get the lead out. We're holding the front page."

The young cop grinned, as much as to say, "Yeah, I can just see me telling Cavanaugh to get the lead out." He closed the door.

Zero had already slipped into Steve Rice's living room. It was long and low, with a marble-faced fireplace in the center, and French windows opening onto a roof garden at the other end. The floor was hard rubber tile.

The room had apparently been the scene of a terrific struggle. The brass fireplace set had been overturned; three of the scatter rugs were rumpled; a lamp table and lamp, a spindly mahogany chair had been upset on opposite sides of the room. The upper curtain rod on one of the French windows had been torn from its support and there was a dark smear on the filmy marquisette itself, as though somebody with blood on his hand had grasped the curtain for a last moment of support. Beyond the windows a flower pot had been smashed to smithereens on the roof garden floor.

Two of the police lab technicians were squatting on the hearth, their attention focused on a pair of fireplace tongs. Zero paused behind them, studying the dark brown stain that was on the end of the tongs handle.

One of the lab men said, "I figure he fell on it. He tripped over that rug and fell on it. Maybe hit his head. If somebody tried to conk him with them tongs, you'd have the stain on the side—not on top. And the tongs wouldn't likely be here with the rest of the tools if that was the case."

ZERO MOVED toward a sofa where Ed Cavanaugh sat stiffly, talking to a nervous, red-haired youth of about eighteen who was wearing the trim dark blue uniform of the Shelton Arms on the collar band—the night elevator operator.

"I couldn't be wrong about it," the elevator boy insisted, his small face earnest. "There's just two apartments in the penthouse—this and the Gaylords'. The Gaylords have been on vacation for a week now. I brought up Mr. Steve Rice and nobody else. Just him and me in the car. He gimme a buck."

Cavanaugh, his dark homely face expressionless, tapped a notebook with a pencil, stared at the youth. "Earlier, maybe?"

The operator shook his head. "Nobody. I didn't make a single trip up to the penthouse except that one. If there was somebody up here laying for him, he didn't come up while I was on duty. I come on at nine. Maybe Folsom brought somebody up before nine, but I didn't."

Zero turned at the sound of heavy footsteps moving into the room from the roof garden. Chief-of-Police George Yancy came into the room followed by one of Cavanaugh's plainclothes subordinates. Yancy was in shirt sleeves and wide suspenders that were baby blue where they were not soiled and sweat-stained. He had a cold stump of a cigar in his mouth. He came over and stood behind the sofa, his paunch creased against the top edge.

"How're you doin', Ed?" he asked.

Cavanaugh didn't answer. He spoke to the elevator operator. "You can go back now, Anderson." He glanced up at the young cop who had been posted in the apartment building entryway. "Where's Ira Rice?"

The young cop coughed. "Gone to the morgue, I guess."

Cavanaugh didn't say anything; he just stared at the young cop, whose face reddened. Finally, "All right, I guess you know what to do. Go after Rice, and bring him here if you have to drag him. I want him, and I want him now."

The young cop moved toward the door, and Yancy asked, "What for?"

Cavanaugh stood up. "I want him to open his son's safe."

Yancy straightened away from the sofa, shook his head. "Ira won't know the combination. You know how those two got along—like cat and dog."

"I've got the combination." Cavanaugh patted the right-hand

pocket of his suit coat. "Found it thumbtacked to the bottom of a desk drawer." He nodded toward the door of Steve Rice's study.

Zero's pulse quickened as he recalled what Steve had told him in the anteroom at the Community Building: "I've got something but I don't know how to use it." Some kind of evidence—of what and against whom he had not said. If Zero could get that combination, or even get a glance at it....

The door off the hall opened and Cord Selmer, white Panama hat in hand, came in. His quick gray eyes darted about, touched Yancy, who grunted and turned his back. Cavanaugh said, "Good morning, Mr. Selmer."

Selmer, clutching his hat brim, advanced with jerky steps. He was all spring steel and fine wire, and his voice had the nasal twang of an out-of-tune guitar.

"Not a very good morning, I'm afraid," he said. As he came to the sofa, the tautness suddenly went out of him, and he collapsed on the cushions, crossed one thin knee tightly over the other. He sat quietly, helped himself to the cigarettes Cavanaugh proffered.

"Whatever it was, it wasn't suicide," Selmer said. He put the cigarette to his small mouth, ducked to the match that Cavanaugh held. "Was it?" he said sharply, after he had taken a short drag.

Cavanaugh was shaking his head slowly. "There was a struggle. Look at the room—that lamp table over there, the rugs, the fireplace set, the blood on the curtain."

Yancy paced away from the others and turned, his hands clasped behind his back, lips twisting into a smile of derision. "Only, nobody came up here except Steve Rice. And the apartment was locked. It's a deadlock, Ed, if you noticed, which means that if—*if,* I said—there *was* somebody up here laying for Steve, that somebody had to have a key to lock the door after himself when he left.

"And the key to the apartment was on Steve Rice's person when they swept him up off the pavement. I think he was drunk, myself, and maybe he fell and hit his head on the tongs. Half conked out, he staggered out onto the roof garden and fell over the parapet."

"Steve was never drunk," Selmer snapped. His gray eyes clashed with Yancy's. "He took an occasional drink, but never to excess. Never. And if that's an example of your reasoning powers, Yancy, it's little wonder this town is in such a god-awful mess!"

Cavanaugh said calmly, "Let's save that sort of thing for the November campaign, Selmer."

Zero moved to a spot directly behind Cavanaugh. He stared fixedly down at Cavanaugh's right-hand coat pocket. There was no flap on the pocket and it gaped a little at the top.

Stealthily, Zero's right hand crept down the back sofa cushions to within two inches of the top of the pocket, stopped there. His heart hammered.

CAVANAUGH WAS saying, "You, Selmer, and the elevator boy, were the last persons to see Steve Rice alive."

"Steve drove me home after the meeting," Selmer said, and he clasped his thin fingers about a knee. "We left the Community Building together. That was shortly after one. Steve was not drunk."

No, but the two men had had a drink in the car, Zero remembered. Perhaps they had drunk a sardonic toast to Captain Zero.

"Hadn't been drinking at all, huh?" Yancy put in.

"No."

"Did he seem—agitated?" Cavanaugh asked.

"He did not." Selmer poked out his cigarette butt. "Excited, yes. Who wouldn't be, the way Captain Zero brought that meeting to a climax?" He uttered a short nasal laugh and glanced at Yancy.

Cavanaugh massaged the side of his angular jaw. "What about that, Selmer—this Captain Zero? It's a gag, of course, but what kind of a gag?"

Selmer did not immediately answer. His thin face was taut, puzzled. "If by 'gag' you mean 'device,' you're wrong. Steve told me that Zero is a man. Some sort of clever illusionist. Probably a professional magician."

Cavanaugh sneezed suddenly. Zero, startled, saw the detective's right hand brush up the tail of his suit coat to get to the handkerchief in his trouser hip pocket. The coat pocket bellied out at the top. It was now or never.

Zero's hand darted down into the opening, the tips of his two fingers closing on the edge of a white oblong of stiff paper, jerked upward, and—

He'd dropped it. The card stood on end on the sofa cushions behind Cavanaugh, leaning against the detective's hip. Cavanaugh tipped back, but not before Zero had glimpsed the four numbers typewritten on the card—4-8-5-2. He repeated them in his mind. Four, eight, five, two. Forty-eight, fifty-two. Forty-eight, fifty-two.

"What's that?"

Zero realized suddenly that Yancy was looking directly at him. A feeling of utter nakedness passed over him. His blood chilled. He took a quick, silent step to the left, felt somewhat better, for Yancy's eyes had not followed him.

"What's what?" Cavanaugh had asked.

"I don't know," Yancy said uneasily and took a step toward the sofa. "Just a second ago there was something right over the top of your head. A couple of spots of light."

The damned contact lenses, Zero thought. They'd caught a reflection from the lamp beside Cavanaugh. Cavanaugh had now turned and was staring at the spot where Zero's head had been. Zero started toward the door of Steve Rice's study. That was where the safe was.

Cavanaugh was saying, "You're seeing things, George."

"Maybe so," Yancy granted. "But if Steve Rice was pushed by somebody, yet *nobody* was seen coming up in the elevator with him tonight, the nobody is Captain Zero. He killed Steve Rice."

"Nonsense!" Selmer jerked to his feet. "Captain Zero was working for Steve. Steve told me so himself."

CAPTAIN ZERO was currently on the move toward the study, avoiding the scatter rugs, aware that both Yancy and Cavanaugh were alert for the slightest sound. Even Cord Selmer was trying to see on all sides at once.

Zero had reached the mouth of the short hall when one of

Cavanaugh's print men came out of the study and into the living room, a heavy scowl on his big bovine face.

"We haven't got a damned thing, Cavanaugh," he said. "Nothing but Steve Rice's prints. No wipe marks anywhere, and—" He broke off, looked from Yancy to Cavanaugh to Selmer. "What the hell are you looking at—if it's any of my business?"

Cavanaugh laughed embarrassedly. "I don't know. We're jumpy, that's all. Just plain jumpy."

The second member of the fingerprint team came out of the study and left the door wide open—which was, Zero thought, most considerate. Zero stepped into a small square room walled in knotty pine. One large double-hung window overlooked the narrow side street. There were two lounge chairs, a desk with a swivel chair behind it, a carved teakwood stand.

The door of a long narrow closet stood open, and inside, on the rear wall, was the black-enameled steel panel of a built-in safe equipped with a four-cylinder Sesame lock.

Zero stepped into the closet. He put a thumb to the lock, rotated the cylinders until the facing number was 4852. He twisted the handle, pulled the safe open. Within was a flat steel box and a brown leather briefcase. Zero took out the box. It contained a number of insurance policies, all issued to Steve Rice. These he put back.

He tugged the briefcase out of the safe, opened it. The first of three compartments, defined by two leather separators, contained a packet of receipted bills held together by a rubber band. He glanced at the one on top. It carried the heading of a wholesale distributor of alcoholic beverages and covered delivery of cased liquor to—he did a double-take—*to Akara's place on Pine Bluff.*

He riffled through the others quickly. Without exception, they were all statements issued to the establishment of Johnny The Turk Akara. Puzzled, he dropped them back into the brief-case, explored the second compartment, which contained a small dime-store model notebook partially filled with pencil jottings. The handwriting he did not recognize; certainly it wasn't Steve Rice's.

Was this Steve Rice's briefcase? Or was it Akara's? Had Steve pulled a neat switch on Johnny The Turk to expose his dealings with the rotten administration of Pendleville? To smash his own father?

What in the hell was Zero going to do with the book now that he had it? It would take time to look it over and digest the notations, and time was something Zero had very little of right now.

Even now, he judged, it was dangerously close to four A.M. At dawn the cycle of transparency would end. He smiled at the irony of the situation. A normal man could have slipped the notebook into his pocket and walked off with it, but Zero could not hide anything.

He sighed, dropped the notebook onto the floor, and dug into the last compartment of the briefcase. Inside was a sealed, plain white envelope. He returned the briefcase to the safe and tore open the envelope. There was a slip of paper inside—an I.O.U. for forty-eight thousand dollars bearing the name of John Akara as creditor, and signed by George F. Manning.

George F. Manning, who was number three!

Across the face of the I.O.U. somebody had written in pencil the cryptic letters *U.V.*

As Zero pushed the safe door to, he heard the sound of approaching footsteps and Ed Cavanaugh's voice. He dropped to the closet floor. He pushed the I.O.U. into the pages of the notebook, rolled the two together in his left hand. It was still too big—as big and blunt and solid as a four-bit cigar. If he stepped out into the room with it, it would stand out like BEER blazing in orange neon in the middle of the Sahara.

Pressing the notebook against the near wall of the closet, Zero stood in the door as Cavanaugh, preceded by the trim figure of the *World's* Doro Kelly, entered Steve Rice's study. Doro's elfin face was framed in a wide-brimmed straw hat. As she always did, she looked brash, yum-yum, and plenty lovely.

Cavanaugh, Zero decided, thought so too. Cavanaugh was trying to appear disapprovingly severe, and he wasn't having any luck.

He said, "So you're Steve Rice's fiancée, are you?"

"All's fair in love, war, and the fourth estate," Doro said. She dropped into one of the lounge chairs. She opened her big leather purse, tucked it down into the right side of the chair, took out a notebook and pencil.

Doro said, "I want the story, Ed. And not the usual handout. Was Steve murdered, or was he just tired of it all?"

Cavanaugh did not answer. He was not looking at her. His dark eyes, shiny with alarm, were fixed on the open door of the closet, and Zero got a sinking sensation in the pit of his stomach.

73

The safe! Cavanaugh had noticed that the four cylinders of the combination lock were turned to 4852. Zero had forgotten to spin them back.

CAVANAUGH CAME around the left side of Doro's chair, taking plunging steps toward the closet. Zero ducked low—the notebook still in his left hand—and dived out of the closet to the left of Cavanaugh. Doro watched Cavanaugh, while Akara's note book flitted behind her chair and burrowed down into her open purse.

Whether or not she saw the notebook, Zero didn't know. Maybe she merely sensed his presence or felt a breath of air in motion. Whatever it was, she uttered a scream—not loud, but loud enough.

Cavanaugh was shouting. "He's in here, dammit! Gibbs! Riley! Don't let anybody leave this room!"

Zero did not know whether it was Gibbs or Riley, but a man loomed in the study door—the biggest, the most formidable hunk of humanity he'd ever seen. Zero thrust his arms out stiffly before him and rammed. The cop was forcibly expelled from the doorway. He came down violently on the back of his lap.

Zero, now in the short hall, sprang over the fallen man.

But now Cavanaugh was behind him and Zero was in the long living room with any number of men. He was fleeing in panic, and beneath his left foot one of the white rugs skewed, spun on the slippery floor. He lost his balance, fell against a floor lamp that toppled and crashed.

"Watch the doors!" Cavanaugh shouted. "Those French windows!"

Yancy was the nearest man to the French windows—the front door was already blocked, impassable—and Zero whisked by the wallowing police chief, through the French windows. Something crunched beneath his foot. He didn't have to look down to know it was dirt from the broken flowerpot. He didn't have to look back to know he had left a footprint in the soil and that Yancy wouldn't miss it.

"He's out here!" Yancy bellowed.

And so he was, out on the roof garden where the freshening breeze of early morning tossed the foliage of potted rose-trees. Across Broad Street and far to the east, the first thin gray fingers of dawn were pushing upward into the sky.

Time was the trap, the roof garden a cul-de-sac. The garden did not, as he had supposed it would, circumscribe the penthouse at all, nor offer an avenue of escape into the neighboring apartment. It was a dead end, a jumping-off-place—for Captain Zero as well as for Steve Rice.

ZERO, FLAT against the three-foot parapet that enclosed the garden on three sides, glanced down the path that Steve had taken into Broad Street ten full stories below. He felt, as Steve must have felt, the subtle sickening pull of the height. He shook off the hold that fright had on him, beat down the fear, turned, back flat to the parapet, hands clutching at the broad stone coping, looking back toward the French windows.

Yancy had his gun drawn to shoot at any sound, and Cavanaugh, Cord Selmer, Gibbs, and Riley stood there, fanning out from the French windows, moving warily inch by inch, crowding in on him, rushing him toward eternity.

"Watch it, men," Cavanaugh said tautly. "Don't miss anything. Be damned careful. He could toss any one of us right over the rail. Look how he handled Gibbs."

Oh, sure! Zero pictured himself tossing Cavanaugh over the rail. Or Yancy.

Soundlessly, on his thin rawhide soles, he moved across the roof garden to the southern end, thinking he might outflank them. But there was Riley, a short man in plainclothes, gray-faced, determined, standing close to the wall, facing him. And behind, standing a little farther out, was Selmer, pale, keyed to brittleness.

There was no way behind them, and none through them. Zero could not hope to pass through their extended arms, their clutching hands. He was cornered between the dead-end wall and the parapet.

He climbed into it, left arm extended on the Broad Street wall, right arm hugging the sharp corner of solid brick.

His right foot extended gropingly, found solid substance down there. Where the parapet ended against the wall, a ledge reached from there on, belting the penthouse. Zero inched on along the ledge until only the fingers of his left hand clutched the corner. Then he let go.

Belly, chest, and quaking knees against the wall, right side of his face against the wall, he slid first one foot and then the other. They might have heard his shuffling except that they were doing too much shuffling themselves. Now some of them had reached the parapet and they were patting it with their hands.

"Where is he?"

"Don't miss an inch. Look behind everything."

Zero kept on going. On the face of the south wall of the building, the breeze grew into a wind that whipped about his shivering and naked legs, tearing at him, plastering him against the façade with murderous pressure that ended suddenly and left him teetering—backward.

Like a fly he kept on moving, and thanked God for his years of blindness—years of seeing with his feet and hands.

The fingers of his right hand trembled around a sharp edge. Not the corner of the building, surely; he could not have come that far. His hand went farther, touched glass. A window! His hand dropped, found the bottom rail of an upper sash, clung surely. He took a long stride, and then he was standing on the sill of the study window.

Was Doro in there? He didn't know, he couldn't see her, he could see nothing but pine-walled emptiness. And eighteen inches beneath his nose, the brass window-clasp.

Locked.

He went past the window, wearily, hopelessly. The next might open on the neighboring apartment. If it did not open, he'd kick it in, break the glass—and cut himself to bits.

"He's given us the slip."

"The devil he has! He couldn't have got back. We'd have seen the doors open."

"Maybe he fell."

"We'd have heard him."

"Hit the street, you mean?"

Zero wondered what would happen it he did hit the street.

He inched along. Would he lie there lifeless but unseen until the rays of sunrise ended the cycle of his transparency? Or if the spark of life went out, would that other spark—that ray, whatever it was, that mote of atomic fire within him—would it go out, too?

Keep on going, for God's sake! Don't think. Inch along and take it easy.

"Look under things. Under every damned thing. Under every stick of furniture. We don't know how small he is."

Cavanaugh, who a moment before had spoken of Zero as an invisible giant capable of hurling a man over the rail, had now reduced his quarry to the dimensions of a midget.

I wish I were, he thought. I wish I could be so damned small I could set up housekeeping here on this ledge. I wish—

His extended right foot came to a stop. His toes curled. His hair curled, too. This was it. The end of the ledge. The ledge didn't belt the penthouse at all. It didn't offer a way into the next apartment. It ended here. Right here, now.

There was nothing more.

Behind him he could hear the voices of the men closing in on him. Beyond them he could see the sky lighting up. It wouldn't be long now. With the dawn he would lose his cloak of invisibility, and they would have a good target to shoot at. A perfect target.

And they would shoot. It would be like knocking ducks over in a tub.

CHAPTER 8
THE COLD, DEADLY DAWN

H E HAD to go back, back over every heartbreaking inch of that ledge. Back to the roof garden. Back to his hunters. And this time he had no hope of eluding them. He could hear them planning—it was Cavanaugh's idea, a simple and thoroughly effective one—to scatter the earth from the potted plants about, so that wherever Zero set his foot there would be a track.

They would shoot him down, then. Or pin him to the floor and hold him there until the dawn showed them what they had—neither a giant nor a midget, but just an average sort of guy—Lee Allyn—clad in white wool trunks and T-shirt.

He was back to the study window now, clinging to the sash rail. Within the pine-walled room, he saw the blue-eyed dark-haired dream in the big straw hat, standing up, puzzling over something she had taken from her purse. Akara's notebook.

It didn't matter now, to Zero. They were waiting for him back there on the roof garden, scattering dirt upon the floor.

They were spreading the dirt upon his grave.

He thought, Look your last. He smiled wryly and looked at Doro Kelly's face. Then, wondering, he crouched upon the sill.

Would Doro give Captain Zero a break? Or would she prefer to see in headlines:

PLANET REPORTER SNARES ATOMIC FREAK

He crouched there, his hands flat against the glass and finally made his choice. He lifted a finger and tapped with it on the glass, a sound too small to be heard by his hunters on the roof garden.

Doro heard it. She raised her startled, disbelieving eyes. At the same time she crammed Akara's notebook into her purse with a furtive motion.

He tapped again, trying to reach her with eyes that she could not see. Then, with his shaky forefinger, he drew in the grime that layered the window pane the empty insignia—O.

She took a step toward the window, stopped, her lips in an O, frightened, beautiful. She did not scream. She turned her back toward him and stepped briskly to the study door.

He groaned. She'd sold him out. No, she was coming back, not quite so briskly, her eyes fastened on the circle he had drawn in the dust. She'd closed the study door. She meant to help him—not to betray him.

He saw her standing directly in front of him, staring through the glass, through him and into the ever-thinning dark beyond.

If there was only time before the dawn broke….

Her trembling fingers closed on the window latch, twisted it. Both hands dropped to the lifts. She tugged upward. The window gave an inch or so. He slipped his fingers through and helped her raise the sash all the way. Then she stepped back.

"It's all right," he panted, and wondered if he had spoken in the voice of Lee Allyn, or just a breathless, anonymous whisper? He didn't know. He got in over the sill, collapsed for an instant on his hands and knees on the floor.

Then he was on his feet again, tugging the window down,

dropping the Venetian blind from its cornice board to close the slats. And all the while he was talking to her, snatches of sentences, in Zero's vibrant voice.

"Reciprocity. One good turn, you know. Akara's notebook is in your purse. Maybe a scoop for you. Manning's I.O.U. All yours. You'll help me? Now?"

He turned from the window. It seemed to him that he had said a great deal, bargaining with her. And she hadn't said a thing. She was staring at the spot where she thought he was, but he wasn't there.

"Miss Kelly." He saw her eyes jump to the right, searching for his voice. His hands reached out and cupped her elbows. He felt her stiffen against his touch.

"I've got to get out of here. There isn't much time."

She swallowed. She tipped backwards, wavered, her body limp. He shook her fiercely.

"Miss Kelly—"

Her eyelids sprang open.

"Miss Kelly, I've got to have help," he said, his voice quiet, desperate.

"Yes." She merely breathed it. "They—they're in the living room. Some of them. You can't get out. Not possibly."

"I've got to, and I can," he broke in. *"If there was something I could carry and yet be some distance from it so as to draw their fire away from me."*

"I—I don't understand."

"If I had some thread—"

"You mean like black silk thread?" Doro turned, picked up

her purse from the chair, dug into it. "I—I haven't any, I don't think. Not black. It's navy blue."

"Measure off twenty feet. Hurry. Make it double strand." He stepped into the closet, opened the safe—it was still unlocked—hauled out Akara's briefcase, emptied out the package of receipts. He came back to the girl.

"Quick, angel," he said. *"The two ends. You keep the loop."*

HER SHAKING hand thrust the two ends of the double-stranded thread out into space. He snatched it. "You're pretty darned presumptuous," she laughed brokenly.

"Angel," he called her again, and passed the thread ends through the handle of the briefcase. *"As long as I live I'll call you that. Back up ten feet. Hurry. There, that's far enough."* He let go of the briefcase and backed away, watched it swinging and bobbing in the middle of the all but invisible thread.

"You go right on through the study door, along the hall, into the living room," he told her. *"Right to the center of the room, no matter what anybody says. You just keep on going. No, not like that—"* She'd started toward the door. *"Not like you were leading a poodle. Nonchalant."*

"Nonchalant? Did you say nonchalant? About this?" She was looking back and her face was tight. "It's not so much what you're asking me to do, it's—it's *you.* Or it's me. It's me believing in you when everything tells me *not* to believe. In heaven's name, who are you? No, that isn't it—*what* are you?"

"A man," he said lamely. *"There isn't time to explain. Later. But it isn't a trick. I'm asking you to accept me at face value."*

An unfortunate choice of words. Her laugh was short and wild. You? What face?

"Please," he begged. *"Turn around. Don't look at me—I mean, don't watch the briefcase. Fold your arms."*

She turned and folded her arms, her purse clutched tightly to her breast, the loop at her end of the strand around a finger.

"Walk," he urged. *"Right through the door and to the center of the living room. Don't let anybody stop you. Just walk on out."*

She was going through the door. Ten feet behind her, suspended in the air, the briefcase bobbed along. And ten feet behind the case walked Captain Zero. Doro emerged from the hall, faltered, and Zero heard somebody—was it Selmer?—calling from the roof garden.

"Cavanaugh thinks Zero might have gone out on that ledge. He's going after him."

"He'll break his fool neck." That was Yancy. Zero saw the chief stationed in front of the fireplace—possibly he had picked that as the least likely exit for Captain Zero—and Yancy was looking toward the French windows.

The two print men were there, dusting the floor with powder. Near the front door of the apartment stood Gibbs.

GIBBS SAW Doro first. His eyes narrowed. "You get right back there, Miss Kelly, understand?"

Doro tossed her head. "No, I don't understand. I'm not a suspect, and you can't keep me here." She kept right on walking.

Gibbs drew a ponderous shooing gesture. "Go-wan back. That guy is still on the loose in here somewhere. We may have to shoot all over to get him."

Then Gibbs saw the briefcase. He saw it swing around from behind Doro as Zero, holding his end of the thread, made a flanking movement toward the door.

Gibbs drew his .38, shouted, "Stop, or I'll fire!"

The briefcase didn't stop. It marched defiantly through space toward Gibbs. Yancy discovered himself in the line of fire and pounded to the end of the room, bellowing, "He's in here! We've got him!"

Gibbs fired at the briefcase, a clean miss that knocked a chip of marble off the mantel. Doro had stopped, paralyzed. But it was all right that she did stop. She was ten feet from the moving target, and ten feet farther on was Zero, swinging toward Gibbs who had stepped out from the door and was pouring lead at the swinging briefcase.

A slug snapped the thread. The briefcase plopped to the floor. Zero was at the door, then, his hand on the light switch.

"Got him!" Gibbs crowed, and dived toward the briefcase. Yancy dived. Riley, bounding in from the roof garden, and the two print men all converged on the briefcase.

The lights went out. Zero wrenched the door open. The patient gentlemen of the press, patient no longer, poured into the apartment like shock troops. Zero let them come, stepped into the hall after the last had passed, and closed the door. He reached the elevator, thumbed the signal, kept right on thumbing even after the indicator had started to crawl.

"*Hurry,*" he muttered prayerfully. "*Hurry, hurry.*"

"Leggo me!" Yancy bellowed from inside the apartment. "I'm no damned invisible man!"

No, of course not, Zero thought. You, Yancy, least of all. But then with the lights out....

"Turn those lights on!"

Hurry, for the love of heaven!

Zero watched the indicator. Eight. Nine. Ten. The elevator door slid back. Anderson, the operator, leaned out and saw no one. He heard the noise in Steve Rice's apartment, and he left the car, wondering aloud, "What the hell?"

He heard a sound behind him. He glanced back, saw the doors of the elevator sliding shut, saw the empty car dropping away. His hand shot out. He shouted, "Hey, stop!"

Laughter, more relieved than mocking, came out of emptiness.

Thin ticking seconds later, Zero was racing down the street. Only four blocks now, less than that. His breath came in gasps. Now and then he would glance toward the eastern sky, rose tinted already with new morning. Then he would glance down toward his flying feet, watching for the first change in his bodily substance. As always at this hour of dawn, he knew the numbing clutch of dread.

Suppose this time he did not return? Suppose he were destined to remain a hunted cipher, a lonely voice from an empty space?

He staggered up the steps of the *World* building, flung himself against the doors and saw, reflected in the glass, the pale gray shape of himself returning, a shadow that gained density quickly as he moved across the city room without disturbing Fritz Schoof, sleeping with his head pillowed on the desk.

The great black dog got up, stretched himself, yawned, and trotted to the door of Steve Rice's office where he stood, ears cocked for the familiar footstep. He began to wag his tail and wriggle joyously.

The door opened. Lee Allyn in white wool trunks and T-shirt stepped into the room.

"It's all right, Blackie," he panted. He stumbled to the nearest chair and dropped into it. "But—never again. Not like that. It's too dangerous. Never again."

CHAPTER 9
POISON IVY

"WHERE'S YOUR bodyguard?" Doro Kelly asked Lee Allyn when he approached her desk in the *World* city room after he'd had about four hours of sleep.

Allyn blinked owlishly behind his horn-rimmed glasses. "Bodyguard?"

"Man's best friend. Blackie." Doro slammed out a line on her typewriter as if she were sore at somebody. She looked tired. There were brownish circles under her eyes—not unbecoming. Allyn hung a hip on the corner of her desk and thought, Poor kid. Poor tired angel!

He said, "I left Blackie in my room." His furnished room at Mrs. Parsley's.

"That was a tactical error," Doro told him. "Fairish has been looking for you."

"Yeah, I know." Allyn's eyes prowled around the room on

the lookout for the city editor. Only six or seven of the desks were occupied. He did not see Fairish. "His telephone call got me off my pile of paving blocks about forty-five minutes ago. Where is he?"

Doro nodded toward the partitioned cubicles off the opposite side of the room. "In Grindler's office. He and Grindler and Cord Selmer."

"Selmer?" His pale brows tightened in a puzzled frown.

"Yes, Selmer," Doro said crossly. "He's a stockholder. You may not be aware of it, Lee Allyn, but the *World* lost its guiding light last night."

He nodded gravely. "Steve Rice. Yes, I heard something about that." His mouth twitched. "He was alone in his locked penthouse apartment, yet somebody pushed him off the roof—somebody described by George Yancy as 'an arch illusionist who has mastered the art of invisibility.'"

Doro looked up from her typewriter. Her eyes were cool and green. "Do I denote skepticism in your eye?"

"You may," he admitted.

"Well, *I* actually *talked* to Captain Zero," she said. She added quickly, "And keep that under your hat, Lee Allyn."

Allyn was silent a moment. Then, "You actually believe in this invisible Nemesis who pushes people off roof gardens?"

"Captain Zero did *not* push Steve," Doro said hotly. "And I am *not* in the habit of talking to myself, and I must have talked to a person last night. He certainly talked to me."

Her cheeks were flushed, her eyes bright. He'd never seen her looking prettier.

"What's this Captain Zero like?"

"I don't know." She absently fingered the keys of her type-writer, her eyes dreamy. "He's strong."

Tall, strong and handsome. Oh, sure! Allyn turned his head to hide an ironic smile. He slid off the desk, stretched and yawned. As he started toward Managing Editor Grindler's office he thought he'd certainly got off on the wrong foot by pretending not to believe in Captain Zero.

He'd have to think up some ruse to change all that. Otherwise how could he approach the subject of Akara's notebook—the one that was still in Doro's purse?

There were three men in the managing editor's office—Grindler himself, plump and impeccably neat; Fairish, short, thick-chested, red-haired; and Selmer, thin and taut. They were seated about Grindler's desk, and Allyn watched them, sweaty hands in the pockets of his seersucker pants.

"We'll carry on right where Steve left off," Selmer was saying dramatically. "We'll slug it out." He pounded his palm with his fist. "Well smash the Rice machine—or smash ourselves doing it."

Fairish and Grindler exchanged glances. This were something they had heard before. Selmer strummed thoughtfully across his front teeth with his thumbnail. His quick gray eyes touched Allyn's face, then jumped to Fairish.

"Incidentally, I do not particularly approve of the jocular vein in which this Captain Zero was handled in our paper's story."

Grindler smiled: "No?" Fairish got up and turned to the door. He put a hand on Lee Allyn's thin chest and pushed him gently back through it, Fairish's red-brown eyes moved deliberately over the other's blond face, taking it apart, patting it back together.

"I'm going to resign," he began softly, "from my position as your personal alarm clock. That means, Allyn, that the next time you feel like getting a couple hours sleep in the morning you might as well spend the rest of the day in bed. I mean, you're not going to have a job here any more. Is that clear?"

Allyn nodded. "I get it."

"Fine," Fairish said dryly. He dug down into his trousers pocket and came up with a crumpled piece of paper that had an address scribbled on it. He handed it to Allyn. "This is against my better judgment. If there was anyone else around here—" He broke off, his gaze traveling to Doro Kelly.

Allyn said, "I can handle it, whatever it is."

"Kelly," Fairish called.

Doro loftily tapped cigarette ash into a tray. "I despise being shouted at."

FAIRISH GROANED. "Kelly had a bad night," he said. Fairish clasped his hands in mock supplication. "Most high and Irish Kelly, will you kindly accompany junior on this newsworthy assignment and see that the wicked female dragon doesn't swallow him?"

Doro's smile, as she regarded Allyn, was bittersweet. "I'll think about it."

"I'm speaking of Ivy Lindhorst," Fairish said. "Ever hear of her, Allyn?"

Allyn nodded. Ira Rice had mentioned the name of Ivy Lindhorst. She was a perfect source of information on all of Pendleville's underworld—someone to handle with kid gloves.

"Poison Ivy," Doro said. She ripped a sheet of paper from her machine and screamed for the copy boy. Then, "who's she clinging to now, Paul?"

Fairish said, "I had a tip that that joint she operates for Stove Harvey on South Vine got knocked over last night."

"Police raid?" Allyn asked, and he drew a contemptuous glance from Fairish.

"Look, my boy, we may have reached the age of miracles, but any time George Yancy pulls an honest-to-god raid on a creep joint that belongs to Stove Harvey or Pete Flosso, the *World* will tell about it in type three inches high.

"This was a stick-up. I want to know who pulled it, how much they got, and was any blood spilled. If she clams up, make like you've got the inside track and are just checking on a few points. She'll spill it."

Fairish turned, went back toward Grindler's office. Doro Kelly picked up her purse, pushed back from the desk, and stood up. She gave Allyn a cool over-the-shoulder glance.

"Don't be anxious," she said. "The nose wants powdering."

The nose, he thought, was pretty well up in the air. His personal stock had not gone up with it. All he'd done was introduce her to Captain Zero. If her vision of a man she couldn't see eclipsed the one of the man he actually was, there wasn't much Lee Allyn could do about it.

He sat down at Doro's desk. His pale, spectacled eyes fell upon Mr. Bell's miracle. He picked up the 'phone, swiveled around to face the mouth of the corridor into which Doro had disappeared. He put his left elbow down on the handset stand, depressing the switch, breaking the connection between the instrument and the PBX switchboard. He was sitting there, conversing with a dead 'phone when Doro returned.

"Okay, Mr. Z," he said, loud enough for Doro to hear, "I'll tell her when she comes in.... Of course not. I don't want anything to happen to her, either.... Akara's notebook? Right."

Doro came to the desk, slim brows drawn down in a frown. Allyn immediately hung up.

"Who was that? Who's Mr. Z.?"

Allyn was chuckling. He tilted back in the chair. "Ohmigosh! I knew it would begin pretty soon. It was only a matter of time." He waved a hand toward the telephone. "You and I and every unfortunate in this office are going to curse the day that device was invented. We're going to have cranks and pranksters yapping in our ears all day."

She stamped her foot. "Who was it? What did he want?"

Allyn stood up. "Just some damn fool who thought he was talking to another one. Said his name was Zero. Said he gave you a notebook belonging to Johnny The Turk Akara. Said you'd better hand over to me before you got in trouble."

Grinning broadly, Allyn stuck out his hand, not as though he had the slightest notion she would put anything in it. And she didn't. Her lips thinned, her eyes narrowed, and she turned lithely and walked toward the door.

"Hey." He flung himself out of the chair and went after her. "Where are you going?"

"We have a joint assignment, have we not, Mr. Allyn?" She kept clicking right along, through the glass doors and down the steps.

"What's this *Mister Allyn* business?"

She said, "I'll thank you to permit me to answer my own telephone after this. And another thing, I don't care to get chummy with anybody who calls me a liar."

THEY WERE out in the sunshine now, but his outlook had never been blacker. Doro Kelly stepped to her maroon Plymouth coupé, opened the door, and flounced into it, avoiding the helpful hand he tried to put to her elbow.

Allyn got in beside her. "Look, Doro," he said gravely, "I never called you a liar. But with this Captain Zero business—well, you could be mistaken, couldn't you?"

"He's vastly more than a voice. He's a *man*." She kicked at the starter and asked, "What's the address?"

He read it aloud from the paper Fairish had given him, and then withdrew behind a cigarette. A hell of a mess. Nothing—but nothing—he ever thought up worked out the way he planned it to.

This notebook business, now. Suppose Doro didn't have it. Suppose she'd given it to Cavanaugh. But, then, she wouldn't have done that. She'd been in the newspaper game too long to resist the temptation of a scoop.

She probably planned to use the notebook as a starting point for a lone-wolf investigation which could easily lead her into a damned neat gun-trap. Or a death-trap. Or the morgue. There was this I.O.U. Manning had signed worth forty-eight thousand dollars. If Akara found out she had it, he would kill her to get it.

Allyn glanced at her cute profile. That the nose was still up in the air didn't alter the fact that she was a pretty neat little thing. If she got into something rough, whose fault would it be? His. You couldn't make anything else out of it.

He wondered if Irwin and Cordray had signed similar I.O.U.s. He said, "Let's see. Irwin, Cordray, and Manning all gambled, didn't they?"

She said, "Please don't exert yourself to keep the conversational ball rolling."

They had dropped into the lower east side of town where the streets were narrow and grubby, where grubby barefoot children played and starved mongrels nosed into garbage along the curb.

Smoke from the cupola furnaces of Ira Rice's foundry filtered the sun rays, reducing the light to a tarnished gray. Doro slowed the car, peered out at house numbers, finally stopped in front of a two-story frame dwelling that had had a good coat of barn-red paint twenty years ago.

Allyn got out and looked up at the local Cleopatra's palace. Cracked brown window shades were pulled down to the sills. On the second floor a draft which could not be felt in the street sucked a gray rag of lace curtain out of an open window, wiping the porch roof with it. The front yard was hard-packed earth, barren except for a vigorous crop of plantain, an empty whiskey bottle, and a tall spindly tree.

"Ailanthus," Allyn said pleasantly to Doro, nodding at the tree. "It grows in Brooklyn."

She was not impressed. They went up the approach walk together, miles apart. She did not require his assistance with the sagging porch steps.

HE KNOCKED at the door and, after a short wait, said, "She isn't at home."

"You hope." Doro's eyes made him an object of scorn. His lips were shaping up to an "Aw, Doro," when the door of the red house opened.

The woman was roughly six feet tall in soft, heel-less bedroom slippers. She was wearing a sleazy dress, pale blue where it was not covered with windblown daisies the size of sunflowers. It was the damnedest dress, and there wasn't enough of it anywhere to cover her.

It hung crookedly at the bottom, showing one big shapely knee but hiding the other. The side zipper was not closed, did not look as though it could be closed. There was not enough dress at the top to conceal one of the twisted, pink shoulder straps.

Her face startled Allyn. There was so much of it. Maybe after you got used to it, it would be all right. But at first it was just big. Not coarse and hard as he had expected it to be. It was soft without being plump, and the cheeks were fair and downy. The eyes were soft, pansy blue. The lips were large and red. There were soft ringlets of pink-gold hair framing the wide forehead.

"Yes?" she said in a voice that made you think of warm darkness.

Doro's glance at Allyn was like a kick in the shins. He asked if Miss Lindhorst were in.

"No, she isn't," the woman said. Her pansy eyes twinkled. "I have no idea where she is."

Doro said, "Miss Lindhorst, we're from the *World*."

Ivy Lindhorst's laugh was pleasant. "Well," she said. "In that case, I guess maybe I am in." She stepped back and held the door widely open. "Maybe you can find chairs. I'm not sure. But maybe."

They went into a room that was dark and musty. The two chairs and the sofa were piled with newspapers and magazines. A couple of tables held ash traps stacked with cigarette butts. A glass on the floor beside one of the chairs contained watery dregs and a dead fly. Ivy moved about, knocking papers and magazines from the drab brown upholstered cushions.

"Here, miss, here's a spot. Lord, what a sty!" Ivy turned to Allyn. "You got a place, mister? Just throw that stuff on the floor."

Allyn threw the litter onto the floor. When he sat down dust puffed up from the chair cushions into a thin slice of sunlight that came in through a crack in the blind. He watched Ivy Lindhorst cross the room, still impressed by the fact that she could wear slippers like that and not shuffle. She turned, smiling, and addressed Doro Kelly.

"Say, give me the low-down on this screwy story in the papers about some bird who calls himself Captain Zero that nobody can see. Who thinks up junk like that, anyway—some reefer you got working down there?"

Doro said, "We report the news, Miss Lindhorst. News consists of facts. There is such a person. I've talked to him. Don't be too surprised if you get a chance to talk to him yourself."

Ivy Lindhorst chuckled. "That's all I need—an invisible boy friend. I've had every other kind." She sat down on top of some newspapers, crossed her knees. Her eyes wandered over Doro Kelly, not enviously but as though she wondered how Doro managed to look so cool and neat and trim.

ALLYN STARED at Ivy and tried to connect what he saw with what Ira Rice had said of her—that she had known every crook in town at one time or another.

Ivy said, "Well, one of you spill it."

Doro Kelly inclined her head toward Allyn. It was his party and she was waiting skeptically to find out what he would do. He took out a notebook and a pencil.

"We heard your joint was knocked over last night, Miss Lindhorst," he said, dividing his attention between Ivy's soft face and her elevated right leg.

"Where did you hear that?" Ivy was frowning. Her leg jumped a little.

"I get around," he said. "I'd like to know how much they got, and if anybody was hurt."

"H'm. You hear the damnedest things." Ivy straightened her right leg, twisted her foot first one way and then the other, eyeing the soiled slipper critically. "You didn't make this up, did you?"

"Huh-uh. I did not. And I know it's true."

She crossed her legs again, went through the motions of tugging down her skirt. Allyn pointed at her ankle.

"I was watching that a while ago."

"So I noticed, honey." She smiled broadly. "Do you think you're the guy that discovered women's legs?"

"I mean," he said, "I was watching your pulse."

She gaped.

"When anybody crosses his legs like that, an artery back of the knee is partially constricted so that the suspended leg jumps with every heartbeat. When I mentioned the stick-up last night your leg jumped and your pulse picked up. If you still say your place wasn't knocked over, you're not telling the truth."

Ivy grabbed the chair arms and yanked herself forward. "So I'm a liar, huh?" Her eyes burned into him. "Is that what you're saying?"

Allyn glanced at Doro, and her small face was tight with alarm.

Ivy was shrieking. "You get out of my house. Get out. No sawed-off anemic newspaper snoop is going to call me no liar!" Her right hand swooped down to the floor, picked up the glass that contained the watery dregs and the dead fly. She threw the glass at Allyn as he came to his feet. The glass shattered against the wall behind him.

"Now, wait a minute, Miss Lindhorst—"

"Lee, come on!" Doro had already started for the front door.

Ivy came at him, striding, her eyes hot and bright, her lips busy with every word that Allyn had ever heard and a few that Ivy made up as she went along. She caught hold of his coat front, yanked and pushed at him, got him around so that he faced the door.

Then she bounced her knee off the back of his lap, and he

went sailing through the door, onto the porch and down the steps. Doro caught hold of his arm.

"Lee, look out!"

A quart bottle of milk sailed over their heads, smashed on the sidewalk, spattered the contents on the door of the coupé. Then there was nothing left for Ivy to throw except hot cuss words, which she handled very well.

She was standing there on the top steps, feet spread, hands on her hips, her head rocking back and forth. She seemed oblivious to the fact that she'd attracted an audience of a bakery truck driver and two women on their way from the grocery.

Allyn scrambled into the coupé beside Doro. Doro had already started the engine. The coupé's acceleration snapped Allyn back into the cushions.

"Nice news gathering," Doro said dryly.

"When she finds out who was responsible for that tip, she'll hit back. Or Stove Harvey will hit back for her. This could be the end of the truce in the local underworld. It could be the beginning of a chain reaction that'll rock Pendleville apart."

Doro shook her head. "You know, we shouldn't have started with Ivy, for one thing. Fairish gave you a wrong steer. We should have poked around the neighborhood a little, picked up some details. Let's try this lunchroom up here and see what we can get—along with a cup of coffee."

IT LOOKED like the kind of a place where a cup of coffee might include anything from the waitress's thumb to a drowned cockroach. Grease from the smoking grill had built up a film on the window that seemed thicker than the glass itself. The counter was covered with blistered linoleum, coffee stains, wedges of discouraged looking coconut cream pie on thick, chipped plates.

It was the kind of a place where the hamburger chef wipes his hands on his pockets, where the customers lick their thumbs, and the slender profit is augmented by a brisk back-of-the-counter trade in nickel punchboards and two-bit lottery tickets.

There were booths along one side. Doro, in her crisp linen suit, preceded Allyn toward one of them, and six male heads on six hunched shoulders swiveled to stare at her. The man at the grill thought he'd better give his palms an extra good scrubbing on the seat of his pants.

"He keeps his apron clean that way," Allyn said to Doro as he sat down opposite her.

"He does?" Her nose crinkled. The chef had turned around, showing the front of his apron. Allyn could see that he was wrong about that, too.

A waitress, yellow-haired, big-hipped, wearing a dark blue wrap-around apron and bobby socks above cracked patent leather pumps, came to their booth and yawned at them.

"Coffee," Allyn said. He glanced across at Doro, wondering if her appetite had survived the assault on the coffee-joint atmosphere.

"Just coffee," she said. "No cream."

The waitress turned and took her hips back to the counter. Allyn's eyes shifted along the row of bowed backs on the stools.

"I'll bet some of them could tell us something about what went on at Ivy's last night. If you could get one of them to talk."

He smiled at Doro—his peace-offering smile. "Your Captain Zero wouldn't have any trouble making them talk."

Doro looked at him steadily a moment, her eyes less green than blue. Then she raised her purse to the table top, opened it, and took out—Akara's notebook.

"What's that?" he asked carelessly.

"Akara's notebook." Just as carelessly.

"Naw, you're kidding."

"You think so?"

He got up, came around to her side of the table. She moved over to make room for him. It was nice, sitting close to her like that. Even in a dirty little hole-in-the-wall lunchroom, it was nice sitting close like that.

She said quietly, "Captain Zero put it in my purse last night. He got it out of Steve Rice's safe."

Allyn managed an expression of complete incredulity. "Then that guy on the 'phone I was talking to—" He shook his head, forcing a laugh. "Tell me it's a gag, huh?"

SHE FLIPPED the notebook open. "It isn't a gag, Lee. There's no other way I could have got hold of the notebook. It is Akara's. It's a private ledger and dope sheet—the sort Johnny The Turk wouldn't want the Internal Revenue Department to get its hooks on. Look, here on this page, listed under 'Receivable after Aug. 23,' an item of forty-eight thousand dollars."

"Minus a thousand," he said. "What's that for?"

"Wait a minute. We'll get to the minus in a second. Look at this."

100

Doro drew out the I.O.U. payable to Akara, signed by George Manning. Its amount was forty-eight thousand dollars.

She said, "Here's the forty-eight thousand receivable *after* August 23rd."

He nodded vigorously. "That's the date that Manning was killed. Then the minus—" He shivered slightly. *"Overhead. The cost of the killing!"*

Doro flipped the notebook pages. "You're right, Lee. Look here, under expenses—"

She broke off as their coffee came. It was half in the cup and half in the saucer. The yellow-haired waitress took her time about clipping a ten cent check, then moved leisurely away, preening herself in the mirror of a cigarette machine.

"Listen to this," Doro said. " 'To Joe Venetti, one thousand dollars.' And the date corresponds with the killing of Irwin. And on the next page—the date that Cordray was killed—there's another thousand dollars paid to Joe Venetti."

"Hey, then I am right!" he said. "And Joe Venetti—whoever he is—got a thousand bucks on the twenty-third for the Manning job! But let's see this a second."

He picked up the I.O.U. and examined it closely. "What are these penciled initials on here for? 'U.V.' Who's U.V.?"

She shook her head. "I don't know. That's Steve Rice's handwriting, though. I'm sure of it. Maybe U.V. stands for somebody he had to see about the I.O.U. Ursula somebody." Doro laughed nervously. "I tried all the names I can. U.V. doesn't fit anybody I know. All I really know is that Steve was onto something."

"And Steve is dead now," Allyn said quietly. He inserted the

I.O.U. in the notebook and started to withdraw it from the table. Doro's hand came down on top of his. Their eyes met and he smiled at her.

"You heard what the man said—your invisible boy friend. Give the notebook to Lee, he said."

"You mean *you* heard what the man said," she argued. "You were the one who talked to him on the 'phone."

"Sure, and I made it all up, I suppose, about you giving the notebook to me. Oh sure! When I didn't know you had it? When I didn't even believe in any Captain Zero? You'd better be a good girl and do what the man said."

She let him take the notebook, but her eyes worried over him. It was nice to have her eyes worry over him.

"What are you going to do?"

Frowning, he put Akara's notebook into the inner pocket of his coat. He didn't know.

"It's like a lot of small fires breaking out all over town, and here we are with a leaky hose," he said. "But there's one smoldering fuse connecting all the fires. Irwin, Cordray, Manning—they all gambled.

"Manning signed an I.O.U. payable to Akara. Maybe Cordray did too. And Irwin. Then Steve Rice gets hold of Manning's I.O.U. and dies because of it. That's four of the small fires around town we can connect.

"Then Ivy Lindhorst starts having trouble. That's another fire, clear over on the other side of town. Ivy is backed by Stove Harvey. Is Akara hooked up with Harvey too? Or is Akara one of Pete Flosso's boys?"

Allyn worried his lower lip. "Maybe," he added thoughtfully, "Akara is his own boy. But how would he get into a closed corporation like Pendleville?"

"Maybe we can find out," Doro suggested. "Suppose we go out to Akara's tonight, Lee."

"We—ll," he said doubtfully, "maybe. If we can get back early." He turned his attention to his coffee, reached for the sugar container. "Where's the spoon?"

Doro shifted her cup and saucer. "No spoon. You stir it with your fingers."

He laughed and looked about for the yellow-haired waitress and thought for an instant that he saw her just beyond the frame of a door opening into the back of the lunchroom. That was her dark blue wrap-around apron hanging on a nail all right.

"I saw her duck out a second ago," Doro said. "Like she was mad about something."

CHAPTER 10
JOE VENETTI

LIKE SHE was mad about something, she slammed the screen at the rear of the lunchroom. And now her feet were flying up the alley, her yellow hair swept back from her flushed and sullen face. Mabel, her name was, but it should have been Patsy, she thought as she ran. That's what *he* had made of her. A Patsy. Him and his sweet talk!

"Me," she panted. "Me and my lame brain!"

He, Joe Venetti, had said he was flat broke. He had said that one of these days he'd take her out of the lunchroom and down to South America to live on a—a banana farm, wasn't it? A coffee ranch, maybe. Something like that.

She hadn't paid much attention because she had known that, bananas or coffee, it was just so much baloney. But he'd sweet-talked her like that, and bananas or coffee, or even baloney, she'd liked it.

But he'd said he was broke....

"Yeah," she said bitterly. "Big-hearted Mabel!"

She stopped at a gate in a high board fence, almost yanked it off its sagging hinges getting it open. In the back yard beyond, a small white dog came after her, barking and snapping. She kicked at the dog. She told it to shut up, and all the while she sidled away toward a flight of skeleton stairs that climbed up the side of a flat-roofed, gray frame house.

When she got to the steps, she ran up to the second story entrance, went into a hall to pound at the door of Joe's room.

He was there, Joe Venetti, an ugly man, short and bow-legged, with black hair on his shoulders, with ears that stuck out like two clam shells. He opened the door.

"What the hell," he said hoarsely. "Mabel, what the hell's eatin' you? Why ain't you at the lunchroom?"

Her lips drew back into a kind of a smile. "Why ain't I at the lunchroom? *Joe, where's that dough?*"

"What dough?"

"The thousand bucks they was talking about."

He stared at her without comprehension, wondering absently what he'd ever seen in her. She was anything but the dark-eyed little cutie he dreamed would share his coffee bean plantation. Mabel had eyes like blue marbles. Just a dumb hunky, that's what she was.

"What's this about a thousand bucks? You been dreamin' or sumpin? If I had a thousand bucks would I sit here all day and listen to my brains fry under this tin roof?"

"You don't kid me," she shrilled. "You got a thousand dollars. Akara give it to you, you lousy gypper, you!"

HE STARED at the big dumb ox of a woman, and his eyes narrowed. "Who told you, Mabel? Who told you anything like that?" He stood up, his powerful arms at his sides, sweat glistening in the dark hair that covered them.

She tossed her head. "Never mind, you Joe. I guess I ain't so dumb."

"I guess you are," he said softly. "I guess you're pretty damned dumb." He tipped forward on his bare toes and reached for her. He got her thick sweating neck in his hands and his big thumbs stifled her cry. He shoved her back to the wall, his lower lip clamped in his teeth, and bounced her egg-yellow head against the plaster a couple of times. Not too hard. Maybe with a big stupid ox like her, you couldn't do it too hard.

"Who told you—" bump—"I had—" bump—"any dough?" Joe relaxed his grip a little, and the first thing she said with her breath when she got it back was "Waugh!" He dug in with his thumbs again, cut that off short, bounced her once more against the wall.

"You—" bump—"talk!"

She was rolling her blue marble eyes hideously and the tongue lolling out of her mouth was beginning to darken. He let go of her throat, stood in front of her, his bare feet widely spaced, one huge fist cocked in front of her face. That *waugh* sound she made was the drawing in of a breath; she made more of it now and keeled forward against him. He shoved her back to the wall.

"Dumb ox!" he called her. "You gonna talk nice for Joe?"

"I—I'm trying to talk, Joe. Honest, I'm trying."

"You're talking," he said, "but you ain't sayin' nothing."

"Him and her in the lunchroom," Mabel finally gasped. "Maybe you catch 'em, Joe. He's a kinduva square—a little guy with thick glasses."

Joe let her go. "Keep talking, Mabel. A square with thick glasses—who else?"

"A girl," Mabel said. "Kinduva skinny, not much of a shape."

Look who's talking, Joe thought. Look who's talking.

"She's got on a white suit, lots of style her clothes got. Dark hair, a kinduva cute face, but not much of a shape."

"Yeah," he said. "Not all behind her, like yours, huh?"

Mabel reddened. She came away from the wall. "You won't forget me, huh, Joe?" she asked, timid and anxious.

Sure he'd remember her, for just as long as it took to forget. He dragged his coat from the foot of the bed, stood up, and Mabel pawed at his arm.

"Listen, Joe, if you don't have no money—"

He shrugged away from her. "Sure, sure." He reached into his coat pocket, turned to Mabel, a grin on his face, and flipped her a coin.

"You keep the change, baby." He laughed. And walked out

on her, left her flat, standing there staring down at the two-bit piece at her feet.

Big dumb ox, he thought.

Joe Venetti went out into the street and got into his car. It wasn't a flashy job, but there was plenty of oomph under its hood. He drove around into Vine Street, parked a little way beyond the corner, and walked to the lunchroom. Things were getting a little hot. He entered.

THEY WERE in the back room of the hamburger joint—Lee Allyn, Doro Kelly, and the proprietor who said his name was Spud. Spud was not a tall man, but he was a little taller than Allyn, a little heavier, and his smile was as greasy as the food he served.

"Yup," he said to Allyn, "I make it a rule never to be too busy to take money. What was it you wanted to know, mister?"

Allyn had his wallet out. "Joe Venetti," he said. "The name mean anything to you? Ever hear it, or know who the man is?"

"Never heard of him," Spud replied promptly, still smiling, not in the least puzzled.

Allyn fingered out a five dollar bill. He glanced at Doro and thought he detected a faint glint of anxiety in her eyes. He extended the five spot to Spud and said:

"The same question—who is Venetti?"

Spud snatched the bill, folded it lengthwise, tucked it into his shirt pocket under the bib of the dirty apron.

"I thank you," he said. "And you're going to get your money's worth in advice. Don't ask questions, and stay healthy. Now blow, little man, before you fall over something and break a couple dozen bones."

Allyn flushed angrily. He moved a step closer to Spud. "Give me my fin."

"Lee, don't!" Doro warned.

"No sawed-off anemic little newspaper snoop is going to call me a liar!" Ivy shrieked.

He didn't look at the girl. She was just a blur of white at the extreme tight of his range of vision. Allyn put his left hand up toward the pocket where Spud had put the money. Spud backed

off, and Allyn's fingers snapped the cotton tape halter of the apron. A corner of the bib lapped over.

Spud threw a short right at Allyn's jaw. Allyn took it on the shoulder, kept his balance. His right hand went out clawing, ripped the shirt pocket, got the five spot.

Spud reached behind him, pulled an empty milk bottle out of a case. On the upswing, Doro sprang to Spud's side, reached up and behind Spud, caught Spud's forearm. Allyn got in a left and a right to the body, jolting Spud, who stumbled backwards over the milk case, and sat down on a bushel basket piled high with empty tin cans. Spud yelped as though possibly one of the cans had taken a bite at him.

"Lee, come on!" Doro was jerking at the tail of Allyn's seersucker coat.

"Yeah, just a second." Allyn stooped, yanked up the milk case from beneath Spud's right leg, dropped it, complete with bottles, on Spud's chest. Then he turned and legged it after Doro through the back door into the alley.

From the door of the lunchroom, Joe Venetti watched the pair get into Doro Kelly's maroon coupé. Under his breath he said of Doro, "Whatcha mean, she don't have no shape?"

And as the car started, he went out, got into his own faded blue heap, and followed.

He carried Doro's image in his mind for three or four blocks, and then his thoughts turned from curves to practical angles. How the hell would a couple like that get wise to him? He wondered if Mabel was lying about the way she'd learned of the blood-money Akara had paid him.

He kept a loose tail on the maroon coupé all the way downtown. When it pulled into the restricted parking area in front of the *World* office, Joe Venetti's right foot crushed down on the gas treadle. Sweat trickled down his forehead.

He'd better get back out to Akara's. But fast. But fast as hell!

CHAPTER 11
THE BIG SQUEEZE

CHIEF OF POLICE George Yancy took the slim cigar out of his mouth and rolled it between his thumb and fingers. He savored its aroma.

"That's a good smoke, Johnny."

Johnny The Turk Akara sat motionless behind his desk. Through shiny rimless glasses he watched the slovenly fat man in the chair opposite him. His expression was neither one of enthusiasm nor disdain. Yancy was a necessary evil which Akara had learned to tolerate.

He said, "You don't come here to tell me how good my cigars are."

Yancy's piggy eyes flicked across the impassive face of Johnny The Turk. "Nope." He pushed his lips out and frowned. "Johnny, I got to close you down. I got orders."

Akara deliberated a moment. "From Ira Rice?"

Yancy discarded Rice with a loose gesture. "Ira don't count for much any more. Maybe you don't know it, but there are a couple of boys in this town that can close Ira's foundry and drop-forge on twenty-four hours' notice. They got the unions sewed up.

"Anyway, Ira is so steamed up over what happened to Steve that he doesn't know where he's going. Steve fought him with everything he could put his hands on, but now I wouldn't be surprised if old Ira'd kiss Cord Selmer on both cheeks—that's how damned nutty the whole set-up has gotten to be."

Yancy drew on the cigar. "On the surface, that is," he told Johnny The Turk. "Underneath, everything is the same. Damned quiet, except for those four killings. Find somebody to hang those murders on, and everything is going to simmer down, just like always."

Akara said mildly, "I hear that Ivy Lindhorst had a little trouble."

Yancy looked up sharply. "What kind of trouble?"

"Her Vine Street creep joint got heisted. Some McGimper got shot, I heard."

Yancy shook his head. "Not good," he said. "Not good at all. We used to have a nice quiet town here, everything under control. Now—? It better simmer down pretty quick," he added, squinting at Akara. "Wouldn't do to blow up now."

Akara laughed gently. "Don't look at me. I got here a quiet little restaurant."

Yancy wallowed up out of the chair. "Yeah, you got a quiet little restaurant. If that was all it was, I wouldn't be here. You also got a room upstairs that has siphoned off some of the best trade from Flosso's and Harvey's gaming houses. That's why I got to close you down."

Akara didn't say anything.

"I can give you a couple of days, Johnny. How's that? Give

you a chance to move your equipment. Then if, when we look you over, you got a quiet little restaurant—"

"My money's not so good as Flosso's or Harvey's, huh?" Akara asked.

"Sure, it's good. There just isn't so much of it." Yancy waddled to the door, paused, looked back at the big man behind the desk. "Nothing personal, Johnny. It's the squeeze. I'm caught in it, same as you. I got to do what I got to do. You know who tailed me up here?"

Akara shook his head slowly. "Captain Zero?"

"No. Flosso. Pete Flosso."

Akara swiveled around to face the door. His smile was broad. "Maybe, George, you bet on the wrong horse. Could be a dry track, and you got a mudder."

"Yeah." Yancy opened the door. "But right now, the papers say it's going to rain like hell."

YANCY WENT out, crossed the crushed stone that layered the parking lot to the black sedan with PPD in large white letters on the door. He squinted against the glare, against the jabbing blue-white points of light reflected from the chrome trim of the yellow convertible parked to the left of the department car. There were two men in the convertible—Moran, the scarred ex-prize fighter behind the wheel, and Pete Flosso.

Flosso combined thinness with middle age. His hair was dark, and rumor had it that he took vitamins to keep it that way. He was proud of his wavy black hair, always combing it. He had a tic that sometimes contorted the right side of his face, and when it did he looked like a couple of other guys—one handsome in a dissolute sort of way, the other old and gnarled and jumpy. Especially jumpy.

There were two other cars in the lot, one which Yancy presumed to be Akara's—its black-and-chrome elegance was typical of Johnny The Turk—and the second an old, faded blue heap with a lop-eared man waiting at the wheel.

Yancy opened the door of the department car, turned, winked at Pete Flosso in the yellow convertible. Flosso did not wink back.

"Well?" Flosso asked.

"He'll close," Yancy said. "I gave him two days."

"He better." Flosso's right hand went up to the peaked lapel of his light tan coat. He tapped the bulge of his under-arm gun significantly.

Yancy's little eyes sharpened worriedly. He stepped across to Flosso's car and laid a fat hand on the edge of the door.

He said, "Don't start anything, Pete. You let me handle this."

Flosso didn't say anything. The right side of his face quirked slightly.

"I heard Ivy Lindhorst had a little trouble last night," Yancy said. "Somebody got hurt."

Flosso grunted. "Well, don't look at me. I ain't the only guy in town with a rod." He nudged Moran. "Let's roll."

Yancy still clung to the door of the convertible after Moran had started the engine. "I'm not looking at you, Pete. I'm just telling you that kind of stuff don't go. That's the surest way to smash the whole works."

"I got a date tonight with Ivy," Flosso said. He put up a couple of crossed fingers. "Her and I are like that. And we're staying that way. There'll be no change."

Yancy's hand dropped heavily. Crushed rock spurted from beneath the tires of the yellow convertible as it accelerated into Outer Drive. Yancy stepped to his own car and got in wearily under the wheel. He could see the way things were shaping up, and he didn't like what he saw.

AKARA HEARD the police department car leave. Immediately after that there was a knock at the outer door of his office and a hoarse voice said:

"Me. Joe. Work the gimmick, Johnny!"

Akara carried flame from his lighter to the tip of a fresh cigar, and then he pressed the button that operated the electric lock.

Joe Venetti pushed into the room and crossed to the desk. Joe's face was oily with sweat and his eyes had a varnished look.

"Who wassat cop? Whaddy want?" Running his words together like that in his anxiety, he clutched the desk with his hairy hands.

Johnny The Turk stared at Joe Venetti. "Siddown," he said. "Take a load off your heels. That was no cop, that lard tub. Just George Yancy dropping in to say it's a nice day. You don't got to worry about fat old George."

Joe backed to a chair and dropped into it, stretched bowed legs out in front of him, passed a hand across his perspiring brow. "I got plenty else to worry about. I—and you."

He told Akara about the couple in the lunchroom and what Mabel had overheard. He told of tailing the square and the skirt as far as the *World* office. And when he had finished he watched Akara spread his blunt yellow fingers out.

"They got the dope on us," said Joe Venetti. "I don't know where the hell they got it, but they got it."

"It's a crime, maybe, to pay a man a thousand bucks?" Akara asked calmly. "Joe, I tell you what it is they got. They got a little scratch book of mine." That was not all they had, Akara knew, but there was no use getting Joe worked up over something he couldn't do anything about.

"A little scratch book I used so I could keep track of where the money goes—not what it goes *for*. Anybody asks you, why sure I paid you a thousand dollars. Three times I paid you. You're my personal bodyguard, you say.

"Why, Joe," Akara chuckled, "the worst that could happen to you is you'd have to pay the income tax."

"Where'd they get the book?" Joe wanted to know.

"Steve Rice," Akara said. "There was a little slip-up." It was not precisely that, he knew, for the briefcase switch had been deliberate, but Akara did not care to admit this. "It could happen to anybody, what happened to Steve Rice. Our boss, Joe, he is a smart man."

Joe's eyes narrowed. "The boss took care of Steve Rice?"

"Sure."

"How the hell did he do it?"

Akara was thoughtfully silent. He had worried about that a little, himself. He did not like the idea of working with a man whose methods of eliminating obstacles were absolutely unfathomable. You did not know exactly what to be on your guard against, and who would know when the boss would want to get along without you?

"You don't know, do you?" Joe asked.

Akara shook his head. "You go ahead and watch them, Joe—the square and the girl. And I'll speak to the boss."

Joe said, "I'll watch a hell of a lot better if I got a gun. A gun nobody is going to connect with you-know-what."

Akara nodded. "I'll get you a gun, Joe. You sit down. You get a drink, and relax."

CHAPTER 12
THE SECRET OF "U.V."

"URSULA VERPLANK," Doro Kelly said, her eyes half closed, dreamy.

Lee Allyn leaned attentively across their little table in the Palermo Club, one of Stove Harvey's dine-and-danceries. It was the evening of the unsuccessful interview with Ivy Lindhorst.

"What did you say?"

Doro's hand went up in a fluttering little gesture. "Don't bother me, I'm concentrating."

"I don't know why I shouldn't bother you," he said. "You're bothering me plenty in that dress."

Her dress was an ice-blue off-the-shoulders number, and those were very nice shoulders it was off of. Her eyes, blue tonight because of the dress and the subdued lighting of the club, warmed with her smile.

"Like me in it?"

"Love you," he said, "and you know it."

She glanced away, momentarily disconcerted. He wondered if she were thinking of the tall, strong man she had pictured in the rôle of Captain Zero. He sighed. There was only one good thing about her attraction to the man she could not see—it presented competition for Ed Cavanaugh.

He asked, "Who's this Ursula Ver-whatsis?"

The nice shoulders shrugged. "Just a name. I keep thinking of names that fit the initials 'U.V.'"

"What makes you think it's a name? It might be a lodge or a professional society. It could stand for United Veterans."

"Or Unscrupulous Vixens," Doro said. "And speaking of same, there's a charter member right over there." She pointed carelessly with her cigarette across the postage stamp dance floor.

Lee Allyn squinted, did not immediately see any unscrupulous vixens until one of the couples on the dance floor tangoed to the right. Then he saw her. Ivy Lindhorst, her tall, full-bosomed figure sheathed in black satin that could have had nothing under it except Ivy. She had just arisen from a table at the edge of the floor.

Stove Harvey, ruddy and blond, barrel-chested in dress clothes, was holding Ivy Lindhorst's chair.

"Let's go, Lee," Doro whispered. "Let's follow them."

He frowned. "I thought we were going to Akara's."

"I've changed my mind. Anyway, it's early. We can go to Akara's later."

He glanced at his watch. It was ten minutes after ten. Ivy Lindhorst and Stove Harvey were making their way around the dance floor. Harvey would pause now and then to shake hands with somebody, to clap somebody else on the shoulder. Ivy was smiling and—well, she was beautiful in a very big way.

"Yes, sir?"

Allyn looked around and up at the waiter and asked for the check.

"Hurry, Lee," Doro said impatiently. She was on her feet, watching Stove Harvey and Ivy Lindhorst.

Allyn put two bills that amounted to half a week's wages into the waiter's hand, told the man to keep the change. Then he followed Doro, who had already started to trail the other couple.

They'd paused in the foyer, Stove and Ivy, the former to pick up his hat at the check counter, the latter to preen herself in front of a bronze-tinted mirror.

"Stove," Ivy said, "I don't like this glass in here. It doesn't do anything for me, with my pink hair." She broke off then, glaring toward the street door.

Doro Kelly squeezed Allyn's arm. The man Ivy was looking at had come in off the street. He was thin, fortyish, with wavy dark hair precisely combed. His dark eyes were fixed on Ivy Lindhorst.

Doro whispered, "Over here, Lee." She pulled him toward the wall.

"Who is it?"

"Pete Flosso," she said.

There were others in the foyer, patrons, Allyn presumed. Instead of going in or out, they merely stood and watched. Pete Flosso's face was pale, taut. He winked his right eye—it was merely a twitch of the eyelid, a twitch that extended to the side of his thin straight nose and the end of his mouth. Ivy Lindhorst took an indrawn breath that amounted to a scream and stepped quickly to Stove Harvey's side.

Harvey turned from the hat-check counter.

"He called me a name!" Ivy gasped to Stove Harvey, pointing at Pete Flosso. "A dirty name!"

"You mean he winked," Allyn said quietly to Doro.

"Sh!" Doro warned and clenched his arm.

Stove Harvey faced Pete Flosso, and for just a moment he hesitated. Maybe he was considering consequences. He pushed Ivy away from him, took three jolting steps toward Flosso.

Flosso fell back a pace, almost to the door. His right hand streaked upward toward his under-arm gun. He got hold of the gun, and had pulled it half out when a short man in a brown felt hat batted through the door behind him.

The door hit Flosso. He went forward onto his knees just as Stove Harvey kicked out at him. Harvey's kick landed on the point of Flosso's chin. It straightened Flosso out, and it thoroughly chilled him.

He keeled over to the left, shoulder to the floor. His right leg stiffened, the other curled up under him, and he lay perfectly still.

Nobody screamed. Nobody did anything for a moment. Then Ivy swooped at Stove Harvey, caught at his arm.

"Kill him, Harv. Kill him!"

Stove Harvey brushed her off. "Go on upstairs," he growled, jerking his head to indicate a mirror-covered door in the side wall of the foyer. "Get Flosso outta here," he said to the man in the brown felt hat. "If his car's out there, dump him in it."

Ivy had started up the narrow stairway. Stove Harvey turned slowly, his eyes shifting about. His smile was phony, and his color had receded, leaving feverish spots on his broad cheekbones.

"Sorry this had to happen, folks," he said. "Go on back to your tables and have fun, huh? The next round of drinks is on the house."

Some of the customers started back. Doro and Allyn lingered in the foyer. Stove Harvey crossed to the stairway that had swallowed up Ivy Lindhorst, and paused there. The doorman had come in, and he and the man in the brown felt hat were standing over Pete Flosso.

"Pick him up, dammit!" Harvey ordered. "Get him out of here before somebody slips on his greasy wave-set."

THEY PICKED up Flosso, the doorman at the head-end, the other holding his legs. Flosso sagged in the middle. His arms dangled, and the knuckles of his hands rapped loosely against the door sill as he was carried out.

"That," Allyn mused, "was a phony. Or did you know?"

"What was phony about that?" she wondered. "That kick in the jaw sounded pretty solid to me."

"It was. If Flosso had got the gun unlimbered in time, it would have made a solid bang, and a solid bullet would have slammed into Stove Harvey's solid flesh. That doesn't alter the fact that the whole situation was phony. A frame-up maybe? Flosso didn't call Ivy a dirty name, he winked at her. A signal."

"That was his tic," Doro insisted. Allyn helped her under the wheel of her Plymouth coupé.

Allyn closed the door, went around the rear of the car, paused there and glanced about. The parking lot was not well lighted but well enough so that he could see a faded blue car parked on the opposite side of the open area. He went on around to the right side of the coupé and got in.

"What was that again?"

"Flosso's tic," she said, starting the car.

Allyn was listening to Doro, to the engine, and for the sound of another engine that would start up on the other side of the lot.

"He can't help it," she went on. "It's not just his eye—the whole side of his face twitches. So it wasn't any kind of a signal, and am I going to hit anything?"

Allyn looked through the rear. If she went far enough back, she was going to hit the faded blue car. "That's about all," he warned her. "You're clear on the right front."

He said nothing more until Doro had threaded the coupé into northbound traffic lane in the street.

He lit a cigarette. "I think it was Ivy that picked the fight I think when the bottom blows out of everything, like Fairish says, you'll find Ivy is the little firecracker that started it all. That was a phony set-up if I ever saw one. I'm wondering about that stick-up at her place last night. Maybe that was phony too."

They had turned onto Sixteenth Street to get to Outer Drive, and Allyn kept looking back, watching for another break in the stream of cars. It came. The sedan with the faded blue streak on the hood turned into Sixteenth, also.

"What's the matter with you, Lee?"

He asked, "See a couple of headlamps in your mirror?"

"Yes."

"Well," he told her, "they are practically standard equipment on your own Plymouth mirror tonight. They were there shortly after you picked me up at Mrs. Partridge's. The car is faded blue, the driver has outstanding ears, bow-legs, a face that would startle a gorilla, and he seems to be an unknown admirer of yours."

Doro said, "We'll either lose him or pick up some police protection."

After a couple of minutes of skewing around hairpin turns they turned into Akara's crushed-stone parking lot. They got out, followed another pair of well dressed suckers along the curved walk that led up to the imposing front door. They were being bowed into conditioned air when the same pair of close-set headlights pushed through the gateway.

Allyn didn't say anything. He glanced at his watch. Ten-thirty. Time was pushing at him again.

AT ELEVEN o'clock, Joe Venetti came down from the gambling room on Akara's second floor, came down via the old servants' staircase that communicated directly with Akara's office.

He said, "The square can't lose, Johnny. He's playing the wheel, and he's about two yards up already."

Akara smiled. "I know, I know," he said with satisfaction. "Then if something should happen to him, there would be a good motive, eh? He leaves with his pockets full of money, he's found dead somewhere with his pockets empty."

Joe sat down in a lounge chair. "What about the girl?" he asked.

Akara tipped back in his chair, laced his fingers across his belly, and looked at the ceiling. "That, Joe, is something else. The boss says both have got to go. I don't know why. They just do. There must be nothing to connect the two murders. It must not be at the same time. It must not be at the same place. And we must get certain articles away from them—including my little scratch book.

"It will require carefully planning, perfect timing. And we must supply an obvious motive so that Ed Cavanaugh will not look too deep. Or perhaps the girl could have an accident—it would not look like she had been murdered at all."

Joe got up, went into Akara's lavatory, and washed his hands. When he came out, he said:

"There was something funny at the Palermo between Stove Harvey and Pete Flosso. They carried Flosso out like cold meat."

Akara nodded. "The boss is one smart man, Joe. He planned it that way. One very smart man."

Joe Venetti tossed off some liquor and felt better. He went back to the stairway, back to his job....

DORO KELLY said, "I suppose you've come to the conclusion that roulette is a great institution."

They were seated in Akara's first floor cocktail lounge, and it was now ten minutes after eleven. They had spent less than an hour in the gaming room. Allyn was richer by two hundred and thirty-five dollars.

"I feel fattened."

She laughed. "You look anything else but."

"I can't help how I look, I still feel fattened. Nobody can be that lucky."

They listened for a moment to the orchestra playing in the next room.

"Let's dance, Lee," she suggested.

He glanced at his watch. "With you in my arms, I'd forget the time. I've got to get to my room by midnight."

Doro stared at him a moment, full lips just apart and then compressed in a tight line. "Who do you think you are—Cinderella?"

The comparison startled him slightly and he tried to cover. "That's about it. At midnight I change into a pumpkin and six white mice." He laughed, and she didn't. "Seriously—I—I've *got* to get back. It's something I can't control. You've heard over the radio, haven't you—due to conditions beyond our control—"

She pushed back from the table and stood, her purse tightly clenched, her expression one of cool indifference. "Excuse me, please."

She turned quickly, her eyes smarting, a lump in her throat. He could be so darned sweet at times, and then again so utterly incoherent and—well, so *blah*.

An hour ago, she thought, as she threaded her way among the dimly lighted tables and toward the rear of the cocktail lounge, Lee had been very much like any other young man out with a girl. They had been having fun, drinking just enough to develop a pleasant glow. He had been animated, sometimes

125

witty. And now, this limpness, this complete lack of enthusiasm for anything except to get back to bed and sleep.

She thought as she stepped into the powder room that maybe she was to blame. She stepped to the nearest mirror and examined herself critically. No. She wasn't looking her best. Tired. Sort of washed-out. Or maybe that was the light in the place, A kind of mauve light, somewhat violet—

"Violet," she said aloud. And then she thought, Ultra-violet. U.V. That was it. She had it.

It couldn't be anything else—not when penciled on a questionable document. Why hadn't it occurred to her before?

Pulse quickening with excitement, she stepped out of the powder room and into the narrow hall that connected the bar with the restaurant and dance floor. There were three 'phones on the wall separated by bracketed plates of thick glass. None was in use. She stepped to the nearest, dropped a coin into the slot, dialed.

A voice answered, "Police headquarters."

"Ed Cavanaugh," she said, her voice low but distinct. "Please hurry." And then she waited… and waited, annoyed by an uncontrollable desire to look behind her. She looked. No one there. No one in the narrow corridor.

Cavanaugh answered.

"Ed." She sighed gratefully. "It's Doro."

"Oh, hello." Cavanaugh's colorless voice brightened.

"Ed, does the police lab have ultra-violet equipment?" she asked.

That was all she was able to ask. A moving shadow above

her became a hand that cut down between the 'phone and her face, that plastered its moist and fleshy palm over her mouth. A thumb and the side of a forefinger pinched her nostrils tightly shut.

She screamed, but her scream was no louder than Cavanaugh's voice saying hello from the dangling 'phone. Another hand, yellow and blunt-fingered and hairless came around from behind her, put the 'phone back on its hook. Arms tightened about her. The hand that burked her kept burking her.

She was drawn back from the 'phone, lifted and swung about, her legs kicking frantically. A door opened. She was propelled toward it, through it, into the dark. The hand over her mouth and pinching her nose didn't loosen. Nothing loosened. She discovered herself trying to scream again.

Don't scream, she thought. Save your breath. What breath?

Her brain seemed to distend. Her ears felt swollen and full, yet there was a hollowness and a rattling somewhere in her head. And an ache in her chest. A pain back of her eyes. A sensation like sand trickling down the inside her legs, running out through her heels.

All of the sand, until she was limp cloth, empty and still....

LEE ALLYN looked at his watch. 11:30. Doro hadn't returned. Thirty minutes before the zero hour, and she hadn't come back. He couldn't just wait there. He had to find her and get out of Akara's in a hurry.

He got up from the table, his pale face showing strain, went to the back of the cocktail lounge, into the narrow corridor. A girl came out. Not Doro. A girl in a frothy pink dress.

He said, "I'm looking for my— That is, was there another girl in there?"

The girl in pink shook her head. Allyn moved along the corridor into Akara's restaurant. There was a floor show in progress—a string of ten chorines swinging their legs around—which meant that the area surrounding the floor was virtually dark. He picked his way about from table to table, looking for Doro.

Finally he went out into what had been the reception hall of the old mansion, through the front door, and into the warm night. He took the walk that curved around the side of the building leading to the parking lot. He stood at the edge of the crushed stone area, his eyes on the prowl for Doro's maroon Plymouth.

The sedan with the faded blue hood was there. Doro's car wasn't.

He walked toward the rear of the house, thinking that perhaps he might have been mistaken about the location of the Plymouth.

"Damn!" he said. He tipped his watch so that the dial caught the rays from an entry light over a door. It was 11:36.

He retraced his steps toward the front of the building. He did not reenter the club, but skirted the veranda and started down the wide approach walk toward the drive.

A taxi had just pulled up in front of the gate, and a tall, thin, disjointed figure of a man had got out and was helping a middle-aged woman to alight. Both wore evening clothes, and the man—Allyn did a double-take—the man was Cord Selmer.

Allyn quickened his steps. "Hold it a second," he called to the hack driver. "I'm going back downtown."

Cord Selmer jerked about, gray eyes discovering Allyn. He flashed a taut smile.

"Ah," he said. "Our Mr. Allyn." He was being very pleasant about it. "And how does the other half live?"

Allyn shook his head. "Too rich for my blood."

"The food, you mean? We have been looking for a quiet spot where we could get a late supper." Cord Selmer muttered an apology to the lady, stepped over next to Allyn.

Selmer frowned. "Tell me, Allyn, is it true there's gaming here?"

Allyn said, "I picked up better than two hundred dollars at roulette tonight."

"Ah," Selmer said, nodding. "I had an editorial in mind—something that would definitely name names and places. How does one go about getting into the gaming room?"

"There's an elevator," Allyn said, sidling toward the cab, aware of the fleeting seconds. "You may have a little trouble, as well known as you are for opposing such things."

"I may," Selmer admitted.

"You'll have to excuse me, Mr. Selmer," Allyn said. "I'm not feeling any too well. I think the lobster must have walked all the way from Maine—and it hasn't stopped yet."

Allyn ducked into the cab and slammed the door. He gave the driver the address of Mrs. Parsley's rooming house, adding that he would pay fare-and-a-half if the hacky could make it in twelve minutes.

He sat with his weight on his left hip, left leg flexed and up on the cushions, left arm up across the back of the seat. He kept looking out through the rear window as the cab speeded down the steeply inclined road. They hadn't gone half a mile before Allyn saw the close-set headlights of the faded blue car behind them.

So *he* was it—not Doro. Well, that was perfectly all right with him....

JOE VENETTI thought, it's like shooting ducks in a tub. As easy as that. Only he wasn't going to shoot the four-eyed square, he was going to bust the guy's skull with a jimmy. He was going to jimmy open the front door, make like a burglar, and jimmy open the square's skull.

Across the street from the crummy-looking old house that advertised furnished rooms with a pasteboard sign tacked to a porch pillar, Joe Venetti paced restlessly back and forth. The short steel jimmy was up his right sleeve, lying cold along the inner side of his arm.

Bust the square's head open and grab the dough he'd won off Johnny The Turk's roulette wheel. Grab Johnny's little scratch book, too, if it was around, and the I.O.U. that rich George Manning had signed. Those were Joe Venetti's orders.

He looked at the upstairs front window as the square, minus his horn-rimmed glasses, stepped to it and pulled down the blind. Far across town a clock in a steeple boomed midnight. Joe turned, paced slowly back in the direction of the distant street lamp on the corner, and then back.

It was a quiet street, a dark and narrow street, only a few lights in the windows of the old houses. Probably a whole bunch of squares lived on this street, Joe thought. A bunch of hard-working squares, and they all went to bed early.

Five, maybe ten minutes went by, and the light behind the drawn blind of the upstairs window went out. The square, Joe decided—*his* square—had got into bed.

"Give him plenty of time," Joe said under his breath. He paced back toward the street lamp. In just about an hour from now, he speculated, he'd be a thousand bucks richer.

The door of the old dump where the four-eyed square lived had opened and closed, and something huge and black had come out into the porch. Joe heard a faint metallic tinkle.

Like a dog-tag, it occurred to him. Sure, that's what it was. Somebody had let a dog out, and a damned good thing. Joe didn't want to bust into a house to bust a guy's skull, only to find out he had to tangle with a dog.

A big dog, too. The animal trotted along the opposite sidewalk toward the street light at the end of the block. A big black dog with something on its back. What the hell? A kind of a sticking-up wishbone on the big dog's back.

Then he knew what it was. He'd seen a blind man with a dog, once, and the dog had a stiff leather handle attached to its harness. A kind of a stanchion. The blind man hung onto it and let the dog guide him.

Maybe there was a blind man living in the square's house. Joe knew that the thing he had to do had to be done before the big black dog came back from its nightly prowl.

It had to be done right now.

Joe let the jimmy slide down until the end of it rested in his right palm. Already the damned thing felt sticky.

CHAPTER 13
THE RED HOUSE

IVY LINDHORST came home from Stove Harvey's Club Palermo shortly after one o'clock. She paid off her cab with the exact amount of change, got out, lifted her long black satin skirt, and loped up the short walk that led to the porch of the barn-red painted frame house in Vine Street. She dug into her black-beaded evening purse for her key.

She found the key, stooped over the lock.

Something made her stop. Somebody behind her? A whispering footstep?

"Nuts!" But she looked back over her shoulder anyway to make sure. Nobody. Nobody at all. "Nuts."

She went into the untidy living room where she'd left a lamp burning, took off her light wrap, tossed it into a chair that was already buried with newspapers and books. She ran splayed fingers up into her pinkish gold hair, fluffed it out, scratched sleepily.

Her feet hurt. They always did when she wore anything besides bedroom slippers. She clung to the edge of the open front door with her left hand, kicked up her left foot, pulled off the high-heeled satin sandal and threw it—she didn't care where.

"You're apt to hurt somebody, doing that."

She let go of the door, stood lopsidedly in one shoe, her pansy blue eyes wide with alarm. She turned completely around, very slowly, searching every shadowy corner of the room.

"Aw hell," she said. She slammed the door. "Voices yet. I guess I need a drink."

She stepped to the golden oak buffet, opened one of its doors, took out a bottle two-thirds full of gin. She put the bottle on top of the buffet, went to another compartment to bring out a glass. She put the glass down, reached for the bottle, but didn't quite touch it. Because the bottle was already uncorked. The stopper was sitting beside the bottle—but she couldn't remember having removed it.

"Phooie!" she said. First it was a voice telling her she might hurt somebody and now a bottle that uncorked itself. "If I have a drink," she said, "the party really will get wild."

She reached for the glass, raised it an inch from the buffet top before arresting the movement.

"This," she said angrily, "has gone plenty damn far!"

There was another glass on top of the buffet. One in her hand, another just standing there. That made two glasses, and she was positive she had moved only one.

"Dammit," she said, "I need a good stiff shot after that." Her left hand, holding the glass, moved toward the bottle, which immediately lifted a few inches and tipped invitingly toward her glass.

"Say when, Ivy."

THE GLASS slipped from her fingers, shattered on the edge of the buffet. This time the voice was very close to her, coming from a point in space directly above the bottle. The bottle had righted itself and sat down.

With an indrawn breath that was a kind of shriek, she turned, fled back into the living room, pounced on hands and knees onto the sofa, and buried her face in a cushion.

Splot-splot-splot.

It was a distinct and, to Ivy, a terrible sound. Gin pouring itself into a glass. Then *splot-splot-splot*, into another glass.

She lifted her head. She scrambled around on her knees, dug her stockinged toes in back of the sofa cushions, crouched there, a lock of pinkish blond hair straying over one eye.

Two glasses with gin in them came floating out of the dining room toward her. They seemed to be following her.

Ivy shook her head vigorously. But that didn't do any good. The glasses kept right on coming. She batted at them with one hand.

"Skat, dammit! Skat the hell out of here."

The voice said, *"I don't mind not being believed in, Ivy, but let me assure you, I'm several biological pigeonholes above a cat."*

She whispered, "You—you're—" But she wasn't going to believe that, and she shook her head.

"Captain Zero," the voice said. *"At your service. Have a drink, Ivy."*

It took her a long time to get her hand out to the proffered glass. When she did, she clenched at it, slopped some of the liquor before she could get it to her mouth for a long, eager draught.

"What the hell do you want from little old me?"

134

"Information."

"Oh?" She sat back and tried to appear coy, but with a face as brazenly beautiful as hers, it couldn't be done. "What makes you think I know anything that you'd want to know?"

Zero moved closer to the sofa. He knew he was going to have to impress Ivy somehow if she was to become cooperative.

He said, *"I think you're a hard-headed witch who wouldn't put a dime on a horse unless the rest of the field had been fixed."* His unseen hand went back of Ivy's pink-gold head. She was wearing a glittering choker necklace studded with rhinestones. His sensitive blindman's fingers located the clasp.

"I think you'll back me," he said, *"against the rest."*

"Why should I?"

He unclasped the choker, and as her hands went up toward her throat, he dangled the sparkling ornament in front of her nose.

"See what I mean?" he said quietly. *"Just about anything you wanted, I could get for you—if I felt like it."* He dropped the necklace in her lap.

"Don't you feel like it?" she asked archly.

"Not unless you decide to cooperate. Not unless you decide to back me against Stove Harvey, Pete Flosso, and Johnny The Turk Akara."

"Akara?" She laughed. "He's small time. He never was anything but a floating crap game operator until he opened that place on the Bluff."

"Then he has got plenty of backing," Zero said. *"Who's Joe Venetti?"*

"Get me another drink."

HE WENT out into the dining room and poured four fingers of gin into her glass, but only a little into his own. Ivy was practical. And she was skeptical. If he could maintain the illusion of a man unseen, invulnerable, and all-powerful, she might be willing to tell him all that he wanted to know.

He started back with the glasses and swayed a little, had to brace himself against the dining room table for a moment. Funny, he thought. During the evening he hadn't taken on anywhere near his capacity of liquor. He'd been moderate. Yet now he felt dizzy.

Ivy had slumped down a little onto the

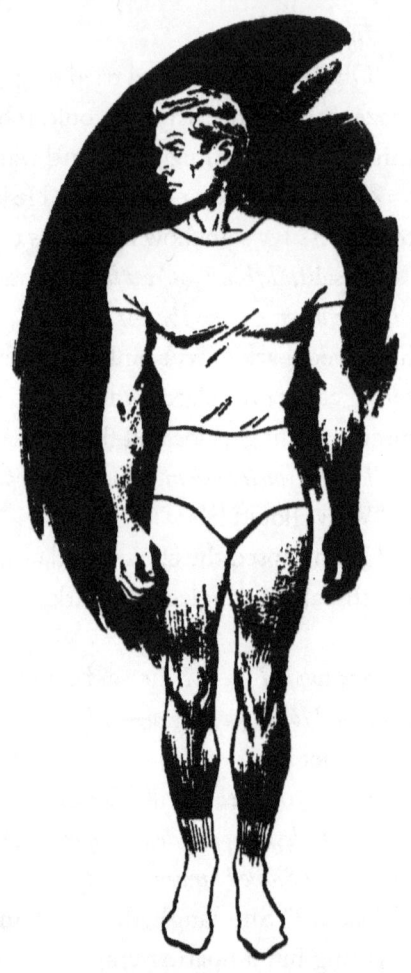

Wherever the morning light found him, he would be pitilessly revealed in his strange outfit.

136

cushions, an elbow and palm propping up her head. She took the glass from him and yawned.

"*You were going to talk,*" he reminded her. He sat down on the chair nearest the sofa, took a sip of his drink. "What about that raid last night—was it Flosso?" Ivy's face looked soft and blank. "Was it Flosso? Or was it a phony—like that business tonight at the Palermo?"

"What did you think of it?" She dipped her nose into her glass and left it there for a while, sucking at the liquor. He was hit by the crazy notion. What if she'd drown? He laughed. There was a muzziness in his head that he didn't like. He didn't seem to be able to concentrate.

"*I think Stove Harvey is a has-been. You're trying to get rid of him, and that scene in the Palermo foyer was phony as hell.*"

"Pete Flosso thought he had a date with me," she said. "Wasn't that funny—that look on his pan? And he called me a name."

Zero said, "*Flosso didn't open his mouth.*"

She laughed.

"*You didn't hear it. He didn't say it. It was a phony. All you wanted was for Harv to take a crack at him—then you thought Flosso would shoot Harv. You want Flosso to be top man.*"

"I'll buy that," she said. She raised her head with an effort. "Do you feel floopy?"

Maybe he did.

HE SAID, "*If you got rid of Harv, then Flosso would take over the whole town. Every joint and racket in it. And Flosso's picked men would head all the unions and dictate to Ira Rice.*"

"You're funny." Her heavy-lidded eyes stared at the spot

where she thought he was. "Funny, funny man." Her lips scarcely moved. "Ever notice this about ivy—it never crawls backwards. Ever see ivy growing *down* a building? Did you ever... see...." Her head nodded. Her glass nodded, too, pouring gin in a steady stream onto the floor.

"Ivy." He stood up, and the room rocked. He felt as if he had inner-spring mattresses for feet. *"Don't pass out."*

Her glass fell from her fingers. Her propping-up arm folded under her, and her head flopped down on the cushions. Zero took hold of the woman's shoulders and tried to shake her awake. It was no good. He didn't seem to be able to lift her, because she was out cold.

When he straightened away from her, the floor heaved under him and he stumbled to the wide cased opening that led into the dining room, paused there, clutching the woodwork. He felt sick, the way the floor was bouncing around. There had been something in the gin besides juniper berry extract—and it was making him sleepy and forgetful.

He let go of the woodwork and took plunging steps to the foot of the stair that led up from the dining room. He climbed, hauling himself upward by means of the banister. There was no light in the upstairs hall.

He stumbled through a door, and his shaking knees encountered the edge of a bed. He wasn't sick, now—only sleepy.

"If I could close my eyes for a second."

He flopped on the bed and closed his eyes. But only for a second. This was dangerous. He might sleep all night and not wake up until noon. Ivy might wake up before he did, and she'd find him there—Lee Allyn in a pair of white wool trunks and a T-shirt.

He rolled off the bed with a heroic effort, crawled toward the door, got hold of it and stood up. He thought, I've got to get out of here. Get out and call Blackie.

He got to the stairs. He started down, both hands on the banister. He had taken four steps before he realized that somebody had turned out all the lights. Ivy? How could it possibly have been Ivy? She was out cold. The dope—whatever it was — had been in the gin bottle. She'd taken on more of it than he had.

He stood there on the stairs, hanging onto the banister. A slim flashlight beam thrust through the darkness in the living room, touched Ivy's glass on the floor beside the sofa, moved over to spot the glass that Zero had been drinking out of. It lingered there, then went out.

Zero was vaguely aware of a funny sound coming from the living room. A crazy sound—nothing that he had ever associated with anybody's living room. Like water dripping in the kitchen sink—*bloop, bloop, bloop.* Like a leaky faucet.

I must be nuts, he thought. He clutched the banister until it seemed a part of him. He extended his right foot carefully, put it down on the next step. The faucet had stopped dripping in the living room. The needle-ray of light darted into the dining room, lifted, struck Zero squarely in his eyes.

Duck! his mind ordered. But if he ducked, he didn't know about it. The world was suddenly filled with sound. The dark was spattered with flaming lances of gun-fire. And he was sinking… sinking… sinking… into a pit of black feathers….

CHAPTER 14
HELL'S OWN HIDEOUT

HE DREAMED that he was back in the Lockridge Research lab again. He was stretched out on a kind of a cot that was more like a griddle with iron bars running across the side-rails. He was very small. Everybody else in the room was gigantic. A big nurse with a face like Ivy Lindhorst, only bigger, came over to him and took his pulse.

She said, "He seems floopy, Dr. Lockridge."

Lockridge, enormous and grave, approached the cot with a hypodermic needle the size of a fire extinguisher in his hand. He peered at Lee Allyn. He nodded.

"We'll give you a little atropin now."

"No," Allyn protested. "No atropin. You know what happened to that other guy. You told me about him. You thought it was the D.T.s. He broke up the furniture. He tried to jump out the window."

It wasn't any good. Lockridge was pumping atropin into him, and he was on fire, on a griddle with iron bars at his back, gouging into him, with a blinding ray of light penetrating every cell of his brain. Light like the sun....

Too damned much like the sun.

He rolled over on the bars of iron. It looked more like a staircase, now and that was what he was lying on. At the top of the stairs light like the sun streamed in through the window to strike him full in the face.

It *was* the sun.

He scowled tightly, trying to remember. On the step just above him were crumbs of something whitish.

"Atropin," he said aloud. Then he put out a finger and touched the powder. Gritty stuff. Like plaster dust.

Somebody had fired a couple of shots, he remembered. He'd been standing on the stairway, and a light struck him full in the eyes. Somebody had fired at the reflection from his contact lenses.

Had fired, but had missed. The bullet had knocked plaster from the wall.

He rolled over and sat up on the bottom step of the stairs in Ivy Lindhorst's red house. His senses reeled and he nearly blacked out again, would have blacked out except for the driving stimulus of fear.

Because it had happened at dawn, as it always happened. The cycle had ended, and his bodily substance had lost its transparency. He was Lee Allyn again, and he was sitting on Ivy Lindhorst's stairway, wearing white wool trunks, a T-shirt, and white wool socks with rawhide soles.

HE STOOD up, hanging onto the newel post. In the living room he could see Ivy reclining on the sofa. If she was still asleep, everything would be all right.

He looked at the figure stretched out on the sofa. Something was wrong. Something unnatural and different about Ivy, or the sofa, or the cushions on the sofa. He stared at the one cushion visible from this angle. It was a funny color, a kind of rusty red-brown. An ugly, dead color.

He clung to the edge of the table and inched his way around

it. Ivy's head came into view, the top of it, or what had been the top of it— the bright slivers of bone against darkened clots matting the hair.

Allyn swayed forward, clutched at the table, and closed his eyes.

Of its own volition, the bottle lifted and began to pour.

She'd been shot in the mouth. She'd been sleep-ing there with her mouth open, and somebody had stuck a gun in her mouth and had blown the top of her head off.

The *fifth*, he thought. *Ivy's the fifth.*

He had to get out of here. He had to get out—but right now!

He turned, let go of the table, and reeled out through the swinging door into the kitchen. He got to the sink, and stared into it, stared at its unwashed dishes.

The faucet wasn't dripping. He didn't know why, but that seemed important. He'd got the impression that a faucet was dripping somewhere in the house. In the living room, where there was no faucet, no sink.

Blood, maybe, he wondered, dripping down on the floor? No. Not that kind of a sound. Not a *splat*. A *bloop bloop*. Anyway, it couldn't have been blood, because that had been before the shooting.

He said aloud. "I've got to get out of here."

He went to the kitchen door that looked out onto a small,

trash-cluttered back yard. Beyond the yard was a broad fence, then the alley. Blackie was out there, waiting for Lee Allyn.

Allyn's whistle was thin and quavering. Then the gate in the fence quivered, gaped open a little. A paw flashed through, then a black pointed muzzle. Blackie nosed the gate fully open, came loping across the back yard, harnessed with the rigid, leather-covered blindman's stanchion.

Allyn had strapped a small bag between the two upright members of the stanchion. In the bag were shoes, sport shirt, wash pants, and socks.

Blackie sat down in front of Allyn, and yawned. Allyn stooped over and unstrapped the bag.

"Where the hell were you?" he asked as he dumped the clothes out onto the kitchen floor, and started to dress.

The big dog cocked its head, first on one side and then on the other.

"Couldn't you sense something was wrong? Couldn't you have got in here, some way, and grabbed off a killer for us? You're going to have to learn to use initiative."

Allyn knelt to tie his shoes, and a rough tongue licked his right ear.

"Okay, so we're pals again. Just wait until I get my specs on, and then see if you can get me out of here without being seen by more than a dozen witnesses."

Allyn traded contact lenses for the horn-rimmed glasses. Then he went back in the living room and tried to remember what he had touched that might retain fingerprints. Eyes avoiding Ivy Lindhorst on the sofa, he picked up the glass on the floor near her hand and wiped it with his handkerchief.

He did the same with the glass which he had used. Back in the dining room, he wiped around the edge of the table. He climbed up the stairs, wiping the rail all the way, and when he got to the top he heard the loud tick of an alarm clock coming from the open door of the bedroom.

He moved into the room. The clock on the dresser said ten minutes past eight. If he was going to get down to the *World* office by eight-thirty, he was going to have to step on it.

He went down the stairs, out into the kitchen where Blackie awaited him.

"Let's go, boy," he said. "Easy now." The dog bounded to the back door.

Allyn opened the door a little way. No one in the back yard No one visible in the yards on either side. He took a firm grip on Blackie's stanchion, stepped across the threshold into the yard.

He was halfway to the gate when a truck turned into the alley and stopped directly back of Ivy Lindhorst's house. He heard the clatter of bottles.

Allyn froze in his tracks as the milkman came striding through the back gate, swinging his wire basket. Then, of course, there was nothing to do but go on. Just walk on by as though nothing were wrong. Smile, maybe—say good morning.

The milkman went by whistling. Allyn listened to the clatter of bottles and milk box. The milkman was knocking at the back door. Evidently on very familiar terms with Miss Lindhorst, the milkman opened the kitchen door.

Allyn started to run....

MRS. PARSLEY said to First-Grade Detective Mahoney that she didn't see any sense to it.

"My lands," she said, "I told all this to the police that came last night. You got the report, you said so yourself, and I don't see no sense to me telling it all over again. Gives me a chill, just to talk about it, that man comin' and jimmyin' the front door like that and pussy-footin' up into Mr. Allyn's room.

"And I tell you, if Blackie had of been there, I wouldn't of had to call the police, I'd have just called the meat wagon. Blackie'd have chewed that burglar and swallowed him. I never seen such a dog."

Detective Mahoney, an earnest young man with prominent and unblinking blue eyes, tried to explain.

"I got the radio prowl car report, see? Now it's my assignment. I got to find this here guy, see? And maybe, I thought, you'd remember something this morning. Take your description of the burglar, now. Lop-eared, you said. Bow-legged. Short. Ugly as sin. That could be six other guys, see?"

Mrs. Parsley, thinking, took a wire hairpin out of one of her gray braids and picked a front tooth. "Bow-legged, I said? He was worse than that. Pot-hooked. Kind of rolled when he walked."

She broke off, craning her neck to see out the front window. "There's Mr. Allyn, now, just coming home. I knew when I did it, I shouldn't have rented to a newspaperman. Comes in all hours, and half the time don't pay his rent." And that dog of his—

" 'No pets,' I says to him right off the bat, but he argued me into it. Says he, 'Some time you might be glad to have Blackie around.' Like last night, I'd of been glad, only where was that Blackie last night?"

The front door opened, and as Allyn came in, Mrs. Parsley screeched at him through the parlor door.

"Mr. Allyn, the police is here."

Allyn faltered at the foot of the stairs. "Wh—what?" he gasped, staring into the parlor.

"One of them, anyways," said Mrs. Parsley, rocking back and forth excitedly in her chair. "A dee-tecative. We was burgled. You, especially, was burgled, and he wants to know was anything took."

Allyn dropped a hand to Blackie's stanchion. "N-no, nothing's missing," he said faintly.

Detective Mahoney came out into the hall. He looked Allyn over pretty carefully and made a mental note that here was a guy with the grade-A jitters. Out all night, so no wonder. What Allyn probably needed was hair of the dog that had bit him. A good stiff one to pull him out of a hangover.

"How do you know if anything's missing or not, Mr. Allyn?" Detective Mahoney asked bluntly.

"I—I—I don't, of course." Allyn forced a laugh. "It's just that I haven't got anything worth taking. I'll go upstairs and look around, if you want."

Mahoney shook his head. "Been running, Allyn?"

Allyn started up the steps. "Walking pretty fast. Nothing like a brisk walk, is there?"

Blackie trotted up the steps ahead of him and the detective followed. The dog led them into the neat, stuffy little front room. Allyn made a perfunctory search of the chest of drawers and the closet.

Mahoney, his mouth open, scratched the side of his jaw with the top of his pencil. "Guess the old lady's yelp scared him away before he had a chance to pick up anything. *If*—" with significant emphasis—"the guy was a burglar. You got any enemies, Mr. Allyn?"

"Oh, no." Hastily. He didn't have any enemies, right now, that he could name—except the police. No use naming them.

Mahoney looked down at Blackie, and grinned. "I'll bet you don't—not with a pup like that hanging around. Do you know a guy who's short, bow-legged, and has lop ears?"

So that was it. The same lad who had followed Allyn and Doro, the night before. The lad with the faded blue car. Allyn made no answer. He was listening to the ringing of the 'phone downstairs, his mind taut. Mrs. Parsley answered it, then came to the foot of the stairs.

"Detective Mahoney is wanted on the 'phone," Mrs. Parsley called.

Allyn, dry-mouthed, said, "Just a second, Mahoney." This could be it—orders from headquarters to pick up Lee Allyn for murder. "I—I just thought of something."

BUT HE hadn't thought of anything—any possible way out. Inwardly trembling, he turned, stumbled to his closet. "My coat," he mumbled. "I had a little money in my coat." He took his seersucker suit coat off the hook, accidentally dropped it to the floor.

He squatted, prolonging the delay, his pale eyes scurrying about. Nothing on the closet floor except his spare pair of oxfords, thick-soled with heavy leather heels. His right hand closed on the toe of one of the shoes. It felt weighty, formidable, certainly better than an empty hand against a trained cop who knew all the tricks of rough-and-tumble fighting.

He straightened, the coat in his left hand hiding the shoe in the right. He turned out of the closet, scarcely looking at Mahoney. He felt pale. Ice water trickled out of his armpits.

"I had some money in the inside pocket," he stammered. He moved around Blackie and close to Mahoney, facing him.

"Is it gone?" Mahoney's eyes were on the coat.

Now, Allyn thought. Now, or not at all....

He whipped up the shoe and slugged Mahoney behind the left ear with the heel of it. Mahoney took half a step forward on caving legs and fell against Allyn, which gave Blackie the wrong idea. The big dog came waltzing around from behind Allyn, snarling, with every intent of chewing off one of Mahoney's legs. Allyn was still holding the coat and the shoe, for some reason, and he was supporting the detective in his arms.

"Back, Blackie," he ordered. "Lie down. Lie down, boy."

Blackie sat down, teeth bared, eyes watchful and dangerous looking. Allyn lugged Mahoney to the bed.

"Is he coming, Mr. Allyn?" Mrs. Parsley called from the foot of the stairs.

"Tell whoever it is that Mahoney will call back," Allyn panted. He had Mahoney half on the bed. He dropped the coat and shoe, finally, lifted the detective's legs, straightened them out on the spread.

Then he went over to the wall at the head of the bed, took down the only framed photograph in the room—one of his dad in the back yard at home with Blackie standing on hind legs, forepaws resting on the old man's shoulders. Allyn turned the frame over. The bulge in the cardboard backing told him that Lop-Ears, whoever he was, had overlooked the hiding place of Akara's notebook and the Manning I.O.U.

Allyn returned the picture to its nail, stepped over to where he'd dropped his coat, picked it up and put it on. He went to the door, snapped his fingers for Blackie to follow at heel.

Downstairs, he paused at the door of Mrs. Parsley's parlor. "You'll take care of Blackie, won't you?" he asked. "There's plenty of canned food. I may be away for a—a day or two."

Mrs. Parsley stopped rocking, stared at him with curdled eyes. "I guess I'll be glad enough to have Blackie around." She extended her hand, coaxed the big dog toward her. "After last night. My lands, I don't know what this town is coming to!"

He didn't know, either, but he was reasonably certain Mrs. Parsley hadn't seen anything yet.

"Where's that policeman?" Mrs. Parsley wanted to know.

"Upstairs," Allyn said. "He'll be down after a while." Then he closed the parlor door to keep Blackie from trying to follow him.

Allyn left Mrs. Parsley's at 8:46. At 9:15 he was knocking frantically at the side door of the red brick three-story building that housed Stove Harvey's Palermo Club—frantically because, on McCullen Street, a cop had called him for jay walking and his pulse hadn't dropped to normal since. A down-at-the-heels character of about sixty shuffled to the door trailing a mop. He had a glass eye that looked twice as alive as its lusterless mate.

"Harvey," Allyn said. "Got to see him." And he pushed through the door in spite of the mop-wielder who was emphatically shaking his head.

THE CLUB PALERMO presented the dismal atmosphere common to a gay night spot at this hour of the morning. The vacuum cleaner was turned off. A man with shaggy gray hair and a rum-blossom nose came over to join the one with the mop. Three eyes considered Lee Allyn. Two heads shook.

"We just work here, don't we, Charley?" said the man with the mop.

Charley said, "Yeah, we just work here. We wanna keep on working here, too."

"Mr. Harvey don't get up until around noon, does he, Charley?"

"Noon," Charley said. "Sometimes after, depending on what he had the night before." He nudged the man with the mop. They exchanged snag-toothed grins.

"Look," Allyn said, trying to keep his voice flat, "I'm a newspaper reporter. I got it straight from the feed box that Stove Harvey is going to be visited by the cops within the next hour or so." He thought that a reasonable assumption since Ivy Lindhorst was generally considered Harvey's girl friend.

"Harvey isn't going to love you guys any less if you get him out of bed to tell him that. And when he says no, it couldn't happen here, you tell him it could—especially when it's murder. Yancy has to at least go through the motions."

150

Glass-Eye thought a minute and said, "I guess you'd better call Harv."

Charley said, "I guess I'd better." He shuffled across the room, entered a dark hallway, and disappeared. Glass-Eye went on with his mopping. Allyn lighted a cigarette, went over to the bar and leaned against it.

He waited... and waited. Pretty soon Charley came back, approached the vacuum cleaner, switched it on, and began to clean like hell.

Allyn had his answer—the boss was on the way down.

Only it wasn't the boss who came out of the narrow stairway that opened on the Club Palermo foyer. It was the Man in the Brown Felt Hat who had assisted Stove Harvey in handling Pete Flosso the night before. He still had his hat on; he probably slept in it. Short, thick-shouldered, with a dry, pallid nightclub complexion, the man squinted at Allyn as the latter approached.

"You're the guy who wants to see Harv?"

Allyn nodded. The other put a hand up and fingered the lapel of Allyn's suit coat. He didn't look as though he thought much of seersucker.

"What's this about? Who was knocked off, Harv wants to know."

"Ivy," Allyn said. "Along about two this morning."

Brown-Hat had one expression, and this was it—like a piece of blank paper that didn't expect to be written on. He let go of Allyn's lapel.

"How do you know?"

"I'll tell Harv."

Brown-Hat said, "Maybe you will." He turned, went back to the door, which he closed. He was gone three—maybe five—minutes before he opened the mirror-covered door to jerk his head indicating that Allyn was to come up.

Stove Harvey's apartment was prosperity's own corner, luxury gone on a spree. That it hadn't a rose marble bath with a splashing fountain and six sportive mermaids could probably be explained by the acute shortage of mermaids.

It had everything else, including white fur rugs, a tiger skin, rich old mahogany and satinwood, chrome, plastics, and structural gloss. Tier tables displayed fragile, costly gimcracks. Etchings. A Van Gogh Books bound in Florentine leather. A faceless statue. A Chinese lacquer-work lowboy and six Hindustan elephant bells ranging in size from Jumbo to Dumbo. And over it all the cold searching light from fluorescent tubes.

Stove Harvey in a pair of pseudo-Russian pajamas of green silk and brilliant brocade, slumped in a red plastic upholstered chair like a crushed Christmas tree ornament. He had an empty glass in his upraised right hand. His chin on his chest, his puffy face had settled into lines of tragic dejection.

Brown-Hat came over, took the glass out of Harvey's fingers, and went to refill it from a cut-glass decanter on top of a French gold-enameled commode. Harvey didn't seem to notice that the glass was gone. Brown-Hat came back, socketed the refill into Harvey's upraised hand. Harvey's eyes came alive and glowered up from bushy blond brows at Lee Allyn.

"Siddown."

ALLYN SAT down uneasily on a teakwood chair, a carved dragon nuzzling his spine.

"What about Ivy?" Stove Harvey asked.

Brown-Hat went to the front end of the room and sat down in a chair in front of the window that overlooked the street.

Allyn said, "She was shot." Then, because it looked as though Harvey were taking it hard, he added, "She was out like a light at the time and couldn't have known what hit her."

Stove Harvey's belly rose and fell with short, shallow breathing. His eyes were like chips of pop-bottle glass.

"How the hell do you know?"

"I was there," Allyn said simply.

"Did you see who did it?"

"No. He shot at me, and I conked out. There was something planted in the gin we'd been drinking." Allyn paused, wondering how far he'd better go. All the way, he guessed. If Stove Harvey had killed Ivy—Harvey's motive was sound—he would inevitably show his hand before this was over.

"He shot at me before he did Ivy. She'd already passed out. When I came to this morning, she was dead. She hadn't stirred from the sofa. I got the hell out of there, and somebody saw me. I'm hot as a little red firecracker, and I'd like you to sell me a spot to cool off in."

The chips of eyes pricked at Lee Allyn's face. After a moment, Harvey said:

"You got a nerve, little guy. A hell of a nerve, coming to me. Why should I take a chance on hiding you out?"

"Because I gave you this preview," Allyn argued. "You got a

better motive than I have for killing her, which Cavanaugh will find out when he gets around to it. Remember last night when Ivy tried to choke you down the barrel of Pete Flosso's gun?"

"That's a lie," Stove Harvey said, struggling forward in his chair. "She wouldn't do that. Ivy was a sweet kid."

"One thing is for sure," Allyn said. "As long as they're looking for me, they won't look too hard at you."

Harvey took a gulp of his pick-me-up. It must have been potent stuff. The whites of his eyes reddened.

"You got a point there," he admitted. And then, as though it hadn't occurred to him before, "How the hell do I know you didn't kill her?"

Allyn's smile was watery. "Now wouldn't I be a damned fool to come here if I did."

Harvey got up from the chair, walked heavily to the end of the room where Brown-Hat was sitting. "Walter," he began, and the rest of what he said to Brown-Hat was not sufficiently loud for Allyn to hear.

Walter didn't say anything except yeah, sure, okay, yeah. Then Harvey came back to where Allyn was seated.

"Walter will take you to Dutch Willie's," Harvey announced. "They'll put you away. But if things get too hot for me, I'll feed you to Yancy. And if I find out you killed Ivy, I'll come on over and take care of you myself. You won't be pretty when I get through."

"I see what you mean," Allyn said, and he moved over toward the door where Brown-Hat was waiting.

CHAPTER 15
HOT BOX

BUTCH WILLIE'S was on Canal Street, a narrow, sooty-faced building of common red brick three stories high. The canal itself, where nearly a century ago mule-towed barges had moved freight, guarded its rear approaches like a moat.

Walter of the brown felt hat said, "Get out, fella."

Allyn got out of the black Lincoln and into sunlight that lay like tarnished brass on the sidewalk. He glanced nervously about, bothered by a sensation of nakedness known to all hunted creatures—the deer away from its thicket, the rabbit beyond the borders of its briar patch, the wanted man in a public thoroughfare.

It was very hot. Shopkeepers had withdrawn into the shadowy interiors of the buildings. Bedding lolled over tenement fire escapes. Four boys were racing down the street after an ice truck.

Walter took hold of Allyn's elbow and steered him through the open door of a bar. There was a brisk trade in cold beer, and Allyn, guided by Walter, drew brief disinterested glances as they entered the stock room at the back.

They went up two flights of stairs, along a corridor, and entered a room where three men in various stages of undress were playing blackjack around a card table. A fourth, bullet-headed, an ugly scar on the back of his neck suggesting he'd proved himself too tough for somebody's hatchetman, turned from the front window, a cigarette dangling from his thin lips.

"Hi, Walter," he said.

Walter jerked his head in salutation. "Dutch," he said. He led Allyn the length of the room, through a connecting door. Beyond was a room of about eight by ten, a dirty floor littered with mashed cigarette ends, a bureau with one leg missing and a cracked mirror. There was a straight chair in front of an open window that looked down onto the canal and there was a frowsy bed.

Walter went to the window, leaned out with the heels of his palms on the sill. He spat significantly and looked back over his shoulder at Allyn. Walter didn't say it was a long way down, but that was what he meant. He turned, went out the door, and Allyn caught the mumble of low-pitched conversation, probably between Walter and Dutch Willie.

Allyn sat down in the chair and lighted a cigarette. Although the door was not locked he felt that he was virtually a prisoner, and that was all right. All he wanted was a place to hide until after midnight. What he would do after that, he didn't know, but he wouldn't stay here. Clear himself of suspicion of Ivy Lindhorst's murder—that was the thing. But how? The process of elimination wasn't getting him anywhere.

He'd thought of Stove Harvey as the logical person to have killed Ivy, because Ivy had so obviously tried to feed Harvey to the wolves—as represented by Pete Flosso.

Then there was Flosso himself. Akara? Johnny The Turk fitted into the picture somewhere—an interloper in the domain of Harvey and Flosso. Yet Ivy, who had played both ends against the middle and must have known the underworld as she knew the palm of her hand, had spoken of Akara as the small-time operator of a floating crap game.

Did you ever see ivy growing down a building? Ivy Lindhorst had asked when Allyn had suggested she was trying to get rid of Harvey in favor of Flosso. Meaning what? That once she had been Flosso's girl friend, and now she wouldn't go back?

And the sound of a faucet dripping into a sink—where there was neither faucet nor sink.

And Steve Rice being pushed off the penthouse roof garden and no one there to have pushed him.

Allyn flipped an inch and a half of cigarette out of the window, watched it fall into the canal. He thought, It's too much for my just-average brain. The answer is there somewhere, if I just knew where to look.

His mind followed the course of least resistance to Doro Kelly—how lovely she had looked on the night before, how she'd be looking right now. She'd be worried about him, maybe— where he was, if he was in hiding or if something had happened to him.

He didn't much care what anyone thought if Doro believed in him. Sighing, he got up from the chair, took off his glasses, and went over to the bed. He lay down and went to sleep almost at once.

HE WAS dreaming that he was asleep in the *World* office, his feet on the desk, and that Fairish came over and looked at him. He could see Fairish standing there, and he knew he ought to wake up, but he couldn't. Fairish caught him by the shoulders and started to shake him.

Only it wasn't Fairish. The bullet-headed guy with the scar on the back of his neck. Dutch Willie.

"Wake up, you. The boss wants to talk to you."

Allyn sat up on the bed, thrust thin legs over the mattress edge, got both feet on the floor. Dutch Willie stepped back, and it was then apparent that Stove Harvey was standing in the door of the room.

Harvey had on a double-breasted suit of navy blue wool crash, a crisp white shirt, navy blue tie, white Panama with a navy blue band. The nearest thing he had found to navy-and-white shoes were black-and-white wingtips.

He had a thick cigar in one side of his mouth, a folded newspaper under one arm.

Allyn squinted at that portion of the newspaper which was visible, brought into focus a head-and-shoulders photo of himself looking—as he always looked when he faced a camera—like a scared rabbit. He couldn't read the caption, and he didn't think that he wanted to. He glanced at his watch. It was 5:40.

Stove Harvey said, "You don't care what time it is. You're not going anywhere."

Allyn pushed his lips into a faint smile. "That's right, I'm not."

Harvey went over to the chair and squatted on the edge of it, knees wide apart. He stared coldly at Allyn. Dutch Willie also stared. He was wearing a ribbed undershirt and a pair of faded twill army pants. He had one sagging eyelid, and the ax that had got him across the back of the neck had apparently sliced a piece off his left cheek. He was not lovely to look at. Allyn's eyes shifted uneasily to Stove Harvey.

"The little white-livered so-and-so's," Dutch Willie said dispassionately.

Harvey took his cigar out of his mouth. "We want to talk to you, Allyn. About Ivy."

Allyn's shrug was sheer bravado, something more splendid than courage.

"I was nuts about that babe," Harvey said. "Hell, I was going to marry her."

Allyn said, "That would have demonstrated stupidity, all right, when you stop to think of the way she tried to shove you down Pete Flosso's gun barrel last night."

Dutch Willie leaned forward, put a palm in Allyn's face, and shoved. Allyn went down on the bed, bounced a little, and stayed down. Dutch Willie rested a knee on the mattress edge, caught Allyn by the hair, jerked him into a sitting position.

"You sit up and take it, see? It ain't good manners to lie down when Stove is talkin' to you." Dutch Willie stepped back a pace, not a very long pace, not long enough from Allyn's point of view.

Allyn put a hand up to his nose to see if it was bleeding. It wasn't. It felt like it ought to.

Harvey said, "When you came to me with that news this morning, it laid me flat. For an hour or so after that, I wasn't using my head. Then I had a little talk with the cops—" meaning, no doubt, that the cops had had a little talk with him—"and I started to use my head. This is the way I got it figured out.

"You wanting a hideout has got to mean one of two things. Either you killed Ivy, or you know who killed her. If you were there, like you say, and didn't kill her, the guy who did knows you were there, and you're holding up to stay out of his hair.

"Now." Harvey took his cigar out of his mouth. His expression was one of self-satisfaction. "Which is it, Allyn?"

Allyn said, "You're not going to like this, but it isn't either. I didn't do it, and if I knew who it was, I'd have gone to the cops." **THEY DIDN'T** like that. Harvey nodded at Dutch. Dutch stepped in, hauled Allyn off the bed, punched Allyn in the belly with a short driving left. Allyn went back to bed again, and the idea was to double up and then let go with both feet, catching Dutch wherever he could.

That was the idea. The double-up part came automatically, but then he couldn't straighten his legs the way the book said. He could tell right away that he wasn't going to be able to do anything.

"You going to talk. Allyn?"

He couldn't say anything. He wasn't sure he could breathe. Dutch got hold of Allyn's legs and hauled him off the bed. He lit on his spine. Dutch picked him up under the armpits, stood him on his feet. His knees started to buckle. Dutch straightened him out with a hard one to the jaw that didn't quite take.

"You did it, didn't you? You killed Ivy, didn't you, Allyn?"

Allyn reeled across the room, ran into the bureau, slid down the side of the bureau to the floor. Vision blurred, drooling a little at the ends of his mouth, he said, "The hell—with you."

"Better get some water, Stove. I think he's gonna pass out."

Allyn wasn't quite out. His brain was still operating. All he had to do, his brain said, was to tell them it was Pete Flosso who killed Ivy, and then they'd leave him alone. His brain said that, and his conscience called him a dirty name.

If he said it was Flosso, Stove Harvey and Dutch would go out and kill Flosso. Maybe it *was* Flosso. If it wasn't, killing Flosso would represent no great loss to the community. Neither Flosso nor Harvey would be greatly missed. Flosso. Harvey. Harvey. Flosso.

He saw the two of them in his mind facing each other as they had the night before in the foyer of the Palermo Club. Harvey and Flosso with Ivy in between. And Ivy had told Captain Zero that Flosso had had a date with her. And, there in the Palermo foyer, she had told Harvey that Flosso had insulted her. Flosso hadn't.

It was phony. Like the stick-up at Ivy's creep joint was a phony, a part of a plan. Ivy was in it.

Ivy does not grow *down* a building, Allyn remembered the woman saying just before she passed out. Meaning that Ivy herself wouldn't be Flosso's girl friend again, yet she was through with Harvey.

He had it now—the pattern. How he'd missed it before, he didn't know, because it was as old as the hills.

The floor shook under heavy footsteps. Cold water slapped Allyn's face, drenched his head and his shoulders. He tipped forward from the bureau, shuddering, wiping the water out of his eyes. He saw Dutch Willie's scarred face close to his, felt Dutch Willie's hands under his arms, hauling him onto his feet again. In the background Harvey was asking him:

"You going to talk now?"

Allyn nodded. "Now I remember. Now I've got it all straight."

"That's fine."

Allyn said, "She double-crossed you, Harvey. Ivy Lindhorst two-timed you."

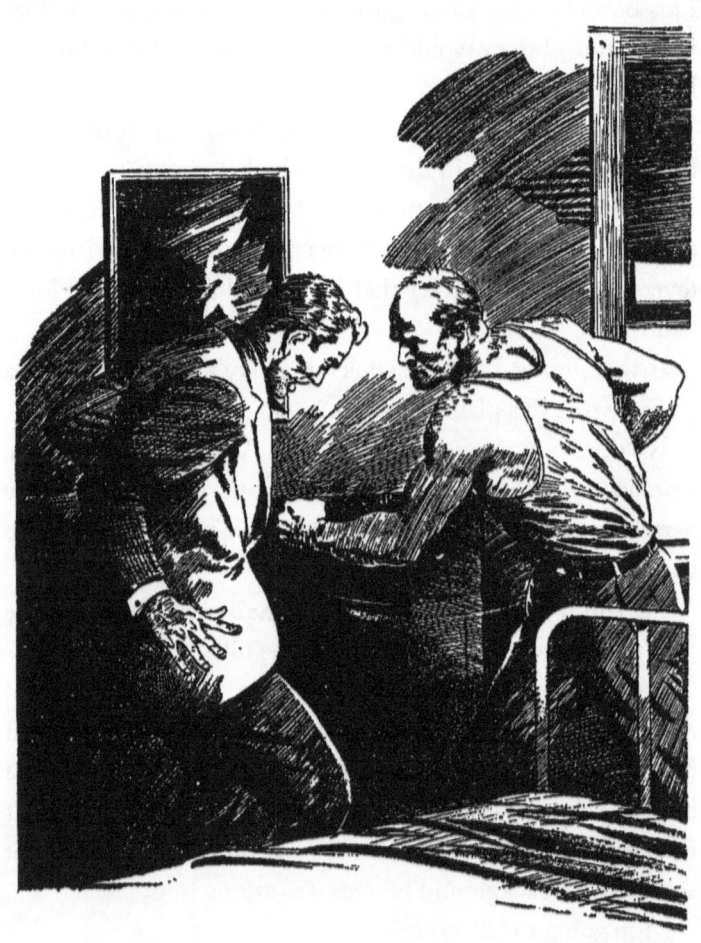

Harvey moved into the picture, a blue-and-white blur. He slugged Allyn on the side of the head with everything that he had—more than enough. Allyn didn't know whether he hit the

"You going to talk, Allyn?" Dutch asked between punches. "You did it, didn't you? You killed Ivy, didn't you?"

floor or floated out of the window. He didn't know anything for a long, long time....

When he came to, it was dark. He was on the floor, lying on his right side, somewhere between the bed and the bureau. The air was hot and humid and smelly. Especially smelly. He thought if he could get to the window and stick his head out, maybe he'd discover something that was fit to breathe.

He looked at the pale night glow representing the window. He was willing himself over there but not actually moving, not sure that he could move, afraid to try because maybe he couldn't.

Then he flexed his legs carefully, starting the dull pain in stiff belly muscles. He rolled onto his knees, hands on the floor, and started to crawl.

There didn't seem to be much object in getting to the window. He didn't give a damn. He reached out with his left hand, got hold of the bed, dragged himself to it and on it. That cost him all that he had, and he passed out again, hands clutching the pillow.

CHAPTER 16
THE YELLOW LINK

E D CAVANAUGH looked at the girl who had knocked at the door of his office. She had yellow hair—not blond, yellow—and round moist blue eyes. Her mouth was loose, full-lipped, and too heavily rouged, her figure slope-shouldered and broad like a pear.

"Yeah," Cavanaugh said in his colorless voice, "I'll see you. Come in."

He'd never seen her before and the hour was late, but Cavanaugh was seeing anybody and at any time. If a straw had come floating along, he'd have talked to it. What with Doro Kelly still on the missing list, what with Lee Allyn still at large, what with Ira Rice on his neck to produce Steve's murderer, what with the Irwins, the Cordrays, and the Mannings giving him hell—a straw would have looked good.

He told the girl to sit down, noticing the sleaziness of her dress and the cheap cracked patent leather pumps that she wore. He could look at her, into her round damp blue eyes, and tell her what was wrong. A man. When they came like this at night, to the police, it was always because a man had done them wrong.

This girl had something clutched in her right hand. Cavanaugh remembered another girl who had clutched something that way in her hand, and it had turned out to be poison for herself.

Watch that hand, huh? Cavanaugh thought.

"What's your name, miss?" he asked

"Mabel Gordon."

He rocked forward in his chair as the girl raised her clenched hand to her mouth. But that was only to cough, not as though she needed to cough but as though clearing her throat would help her clear her mind.

She said, "I work in a lunchroom on Vine Street."

Ivy Lindhorst's neighborhood. That, Cavanaugh told himself pessimistically, needn't mean anything.

"I met a man there name of Joe Venetti."

"Works there, does he?" Cavanaugh asked.

She shook her head slowly, staring off into space. "He was

just hanging around one time." She looked at him, then. "You know Joe Venetti?"

He shook his head. "Boy friend?"

Her eyes dropped. "No," she said tonelessly.

Not any more, Cavanaugh mentally supplied.

"This Joe, he's in trouble," she said, not looking at Cavanaugh. "I think he killed somebody, the way he acted when I told him what I'd heard two people talking about one day in the lunchroom. They were saying that Joe got a thousand dollars from Akara. I think that's what it was—for killing somebody. The twenty-third of this month, they said."

The twenty-third. *Manning! George Manning II!*

"Wait a minute," Cavanaugh said, as much to himself as to the girl. He smiled woodenly. "Just a minute, Miss Gordon. You overheard somebody in the lunchroom talking about Joe Venetti, is that it?"

She nodded. "They—had a notebook. It was full of figures and dates and stuff. They were talking about Joe getting a thousand dollars from Akara. They mentioned some names. Some name like—" She frowned—"like corduroy, the stuff they make pants out of, only that wasn't it."

"Cordray?" Cavanaugh breathed.

THE GIRL nodded. "That's it. That name and another date and Joe got another thousand dollars from Mr. Akara. Joe, he—" She looked down at her clenched fist again—"He owed me some money," she went on faintly. "I went to him for it, he said he was broke, and I asked him what about the thousand dollars he got from Mr. Akara. He went kind of wild."

Mabel raised her left hand, touching her throat, and Cavanaugh noticed the bruises.

She said, "He made me tell him about this couple I overheard talking there in the lunchroom."

Cavanaugh said, "All right, Miss Gordon. Let's get some of this down." He hitched himself around to the desk. "Can you describe Joe Venetti?"

She nodded, space-staring. "He's short, but built awful strong. Real dark. His ears kind of stand out. He's not handsome, exactly, but he wears good clothes."

"Bow-legged, maybe?" Cavanaugh wasn't writing anything. He was looking over a sheet of flimsy—a copy of a police report on an attempted burglary at a lodging house owned by Mrs. Parsley. Lee Allyn lived at the Parsley house.

He swung around to the girl. "How about the pair in the lunchroom. The—uh, square—is that what you called him?"

"A real blondy guy," Mabel told him. "Small and thin, kind of pale eyes and horn-rimmed glasses and kind of weak."

Cavanaugh took a slow, careful breath as though he were dreaming and didn't want to wake himself up.

"The girl," Mabel was saying, "was thin and had short dark hair, and I think her eyes were blue, or maybe green. Kind of a cute face."

Kind of a beautiful face, you mean, Cavanaugh thought. Doro Kelly and Lee Allyn. And between them, some way, they'd got hold of a notebook belonging to Johnny The Turk. From the briefcase in Steve Rice's safe, that's where they had got it. Doro must have got it from there, while Cavanaugh and the others had been trying to trap Captain Zero.

And Steve Rice, who must have obtained the notebook for use in a newspaper exposé of Johnny Akara, had been killed for possessing it. Doro had the notebook now. And Doro was missing....

In spite of the heat, Cavanaugh shivered. He put out a hand to the intercom box, switched to the detective's room. "Mahoney," he said. Turning to Mabel, "I'm going to have to hold you."

"Why?" she gasped fearfully. "I just tried to help."

"Protective custody," Cavanaugh smiled. He looked toward the door as Mahoney came in. "How's the head?"

Mahoney fingered a goose-egg behind his left ear. "I feel like I had two of them."

Cavanaugh said, "That's fine, you'll need two. We want Johnny The Turk. Take Schlemke and Riley. And while you're up there on the Bluff, you might look around for a lop-eared, bow-legged guy, name of Joe Venetti. Looks like he's the boy you're after for the Parsley burglary."

Cavanaugh turned to Mabel Gordon when Mahoney had gone out. "Protective custody," he said kindly. "No charge. We just don't want anything to happen to you." His eyes dropped to Mabel's clenched right hand. "And would you mind showing me what you've got there?"

Mabel's cheeks reddened. Her plump hand opened slowly. "Just a—two-bit piece."

Cavanaugh didn't get it.

After he'd turned Mabel over to a matron, Cavanaugh went

into the adjoining office of the chief of police. Old Ira Rice was there where he had been at least half of the time since Steve Rice had been killed. Cavanaugh looked from the silver-haired boss of Pendleville to fat George Yancy, and smiled a tight little smile.

"I think we've got something."

Yancy took his feet off the scarred desk and his chair squawked forward. His piggy eyes blinked uneasily.

"What have you got?" Ira demanded stridently.

"A link," Cavanaugh said, "connecting Irwin, Cordray, Manning, and—" He paused, nodding at Ira—"and Steve."

"Is that all?" Ira crabbed.

"It isn't much," Cavanaugh said, "or it may be the whole thing. It's beginning. When we get Akara in here, we may have it made."

Ira grunted. "If you'd stopped all that tomfoolery about looking for this Zero person you can't even see, you'd have made a little real progress." He shot out a finger at Yancy. "I told you, didn't I, that Zero couldn't have killed Steve? Zero was at my place when it happened."

Cavanaugh hadn't heard this. He looked at George Yancy. The chief of police forced a laugh.

"You can't alibi a man you can't see, Ira. You heard a voice, maybe—"

"I saw his damned impression in a chair in my own home!" Ira shouted. "I saw him pick up a gun."

"Maybe you did," Yancy said. "But if it wasn't Zero who pushed Steve, then Steve wasn't pushed. *There was nobody up in that penthouse except Steve—unless Zero was up there.*"

169

Yancy tipped back in his chair again, his smile ugly, triumphant. "You figure out any other solution if you can. I'd sure as hell like to hear it!"

CHAPTER 17
DOUBLE-CROSS

LEE ALLYN opened his eyes. A cold bright shaft of moonlight slanted through the window of his prison-hideout on Dutch Willie's third floor. In the next room, a card game was in progress. Allyn could hear the occasional mumble of voices, and the click of the chips on the table.

He sat up in bed. He didn't know how it would be when he got his feet on the floor, but sitting up he felt pretty good. Except for his headache. He raised his right hand toward his head, arresting the movement twelve inches or so from his eyes. For an instant he stared, open-mouthed, at the silhouette of his arm against the glow from the window.

There was no visible hand at the end of the sleeve of his seersucker coat.

"Good lord!" he breathed faintly. It had happened again. He had slept through midnight, through the zero hour, and it had happened. He swung his legs around, got his feet down on the floor, stripped off his suit coat, started to fumble with shirt buttons.

No, wait, his mind dictated. Take it easy. Your eyes first.

His shaking hand plunged into the pocket of his suit coat. Where were the contact lenses? If they were broken, if he had to wear glasses instead, that would be exactly like asking for a bullet between the eyes. He tried another pocket, brought out the vial and the lenses intact.

When he'd taken care of the lenses, he removed his outer garments, traded the rayon socks that he wore for the woolen ones with the rawhide soles. Invisible now, he crossed to the bureau, got his horn-rimmed glasses, encased them and put them in the pocket of his seersucker coat. He made a bundle of his clothes, securing it tightly with his belt.

And now what to do? To leave his clothes there was a dead giveaway. He didn't like the idea of throwing them out the window and into the canal, but nothing else occurred to him until he got over to the window. There he stooped, thrust his head and shoulder out, and looked up. The eaves weren't far away, maybe not too far away.

He straightened, quietly lowered the top sash and then the upper one. He gripped the slack end of the belt securing his clothing in his teeth, and backed to the window. He reached up to the top of the frame, got one heel on the sill, and boosted himself up and out through the opening.

Then he was sitting on the top rails of both sashes, half out of the window. He held on to the inner side of the frame with his left hand, got the bundle of clothes by the belt end in his right, hauled the bundle out through the window. On the second swing, the bundle of clothes landed on the eaves, the end of the belt hanging down six or eight inches.

He got down from the window, quietly crossed to the door. He didn't think it was locked, but with those card players out

there, it might just as well have been. If he took the risk of opening the door to make a dash for it, his secret would be out and
Lee Allyn, the visible, would never know another moment of
peace.

He crouched and looked through the keyhole. He could see
Stove Harvey there at the table, playing his cards close to his
barrel of a chest. There were three or four others—he couldn't
be sure of the number.

Stove Harvey's mouth quirked. "I'm out," he growled and
threw down his cards. He stood, stretching, and said, "I guess
I'll go see how my boy is doing in there."

He started toward the door behind which Zero crouched, but
paused as the door on the hall was opened and Dutch Willie
put his bullet-shaped head into the room.

"Spig's here, Stove."

Somebody at the table said, "That damned stool! Don't trust
that guy Spig, Harv."

"Spig's got something," Dutch Willie said.

"Yeah, bugs in his chest!"

Harvey drew an impatient gesture. "I'll see him," he said to
Dutch, and returned to the table for a cigar which he took out
of an ash tray.

"You're off your nut if you trust Spig," one of the players said.

"Will you shut up!" Harvey turned on the speaker. "I've been
running this mob for several years now, and we always done all
right without any advice from you. Sure, Spig is shifty, but I'll
take care of him. I'll take care of him good."

DUTCH WILLIE came back into the room with a gaunt

hollow-chested man wearing baggy gray pants, a dark brown shirt, and a vest with no buttons on it. Dutch stayed at the door while the other took shambling steps toward Stove Harvey.

"Stove, I got something—something I guess you'd like to hear." The voice was frail, whining.

"Yeah?" Harvey said quietly, his face immobile. "What you got, Spig?"

Spig took off his greasy hat and twisted it. His lips curved into an ingratiating smile. "I got to have something for it, Stove."

"You'll get something, if it's any good."

"Fifty dollars?" Spig ventured. "It's about Ivy."

"If it's any good, yes. Go-wan, spill it."

"Last night," Spig began, "it was so damn hot and my cough was so bad I couldn't sleep. I went down into Vine Street, walked along to the corner, and I seen a yellow Packard and Moran at the wheel. It was parked there at the corner, waitin' for somebody, see?"

Harvey nodded. "That all?"

"All?" Spig started to laugh, but the laugh turned into a cough that doubled him up. After the paroxysm, he pulled out a dirty handkerchief and mopped his perspiring face. He touched his lips with the handkerchief, looked at it, put it back in his pocket.

"I kept on up the street, past where Moran was. It was about two in the morning, I guess. I'd just passed Ivy Lindhorst's house when the door opened and a guy came out. In a hurry, see, starting to run toward the corner. Moran turned on the car lights, and I got a good look at the guy. It was Pete Flosso, so help me."

Harvey didn't say anything. He turned his back on Spig,

walked across the room beyond Zero's range of vision. There was the sound of a 'phone being dialed, then Harvey's voice.

"Walter? I'm at Dutch Willie's. Bring the old Caddy."

Harvey hung up, came back to where Spig was waiting. "Where's Flosso now? Do you know?"

"At his place on the river. Him, and Moran, and Selig, maybe a coupla others." Spig put out his hand, rubbed thumb and fore-finger together. "How's about the fifty, Stove?"

Harvey grunted. "You'll get it if this is any good. But you've got to prove it's good, see? You're going with us."

Spig's grin faded. "Pete never liked me."

Harvey laughed softly. "I got news for you, chum. I never liked you, either."

"He'll kill me. I can't go out there," Spig started to back away, but Harvey caught and held him by the loose flaps of his vest.

"If he kills you, Spig, you can be damned sure of one thing—he won't kill nobody else."

A big, golden-haired man at the table laughed. "Don't that make you feel good all over, Spig? Why, you're just like a hero! Stove will maybe give you a medal post-humorously."

Harvey shoved Spig into Dutch Willie's arms, turned to the group at the table, "You guys get your ammo and let's go. If we got to fix Flosso, we got to do it so he stays fixed."

Zero, at the keyhole, saw three men get up from the table and file out of the room. The golden-haired man remained, idly shuffling cards. Stove Harvey paced back and forth. Once he stopped in front of Spig and laughed in the lunger's face.

Dutch Willie said, "You sure you know what you're doing, Harv?"

Harvey didn't answer. His big face was grim, as though maybe he wasn't sure what he would do except that he'd play his cards as they were dealt. Maybe he suspected that this was all a set-up to pit him against Flosso, yet he seemed nevertheless willing to push, bullheaded, on into the trap, looking for the showdown which might enable him to take over the whole town.

He hauled out his under-arm gun, pumped the slide, set the safety, put the automatic back. His eyes stirred restlessly.

"We'd just as well go down. Walter will be here by the time we reach the street. Goldie, you keep an eye on my boy in there." Harvey jerked his head to indicate the door behind which Zero was crouching. Then he, Dutch Willie, and Spig went out of the room.

The big, fair-haired man got up from the table and started toward the small room where Zero waited. One of Goldie's legs was shorter than the other, and he wore a heavy built-up shoe that thumped the floor with every other step.

Zero straightened, his hands clenched, realizing that if Goldie locked the door Zero effectively would be put out of the picture. To open the door before Goldie reached it would instantly betray his presence.

ZERO STOOD there, facing the door. He saw the knob turn. The door swung back, and Goldie stared into the apparently empty room. Alarm spread across the big man's face. He turned, open-mouthed, possibly intending to call Stove Harvey, but before he could utter a sound Zero's left arm hooked around the other's neck.

"Maybe you don't know it," Zero whispered in Goldie's ear, "but you can't live with a ruptured larynx."

Goldie kicked backward with the heavy built-up shoe. It was a frantic move, unaimed but effective. Pain shot through Zero's right leg. His arm relaxed for an instant, and Goldie squirmed around and swung wildly with his right—a blow driven by stark terror.

The blow landed just below Zero's ribs on the left side.

Zero reeled into the door-frame, shoved away from it, lunged at Goldie. His left hand dug into Goldie's throat. His right pounded into the side of Goldie's head. They rocked back together, fell, Zero on top. Goldie's built-up shoe beating on the floor.

Zero kept his stranglehold on Goldie's throat, sent blow after blow into the side of Goldie's head, until finally Goldie wasn't kicking the floor any more.

Zero stood, straddling the unconscious man, wind gone, muscles quivering. Then he staggered to the door, went down deserted stairs, through the stockroom and bar to the street door. The door was closed. Harvey and his mob were on the sidewalk waiting for the car. To open the tavern door would have been a dead giveaway. Zero could only stand and watch through the filmy glass.

Harvey said, "All set?" trying to make it sound cheerful. When nobody answered, Harvey asked, "What's wrong with you guys—you gone yellah?"

176

A kid of not over twenty flipped his cigarette into the gutter. "I just don't like it, that's all. Your doll gets knocked off, so you gotta rip apart the town. What the hell, there's other dolls, ain't there?"

"So you're yellah, huh?"

"Naw, I just don't like it."

A black sedan rounded the corner and pulled up to the curb. Zero noticed to his satisfaction that it was an old car with running boards. Harvey opened the front and rear doors, shoved Spig into the car alongside the driver.

"Get in, you guys."

Two of them got into the back seat, but not the kid who'd said he didn't like it. Harvey looked at him and then at Dutch Willie.

"You going. Dutch?"

"Sure. I was waitin' on Louie." Dutch hooked a thumb at the kid who hung back, and then, at a nod from Harvey, he got into the car.

"You don't have to go, Louie," Harvey said softly. "I don't want to make nobody go. This ain't the draft. You can stay right here if you want to."

The kid looked down at the sidewalk, drew an invisible design with the toe of his shoe. He spat as if he was pretty tough.

"I guess I won't go, then, if it's all right with you, Harv."

"Sure, it's all right with me."

The kid turned, started walking away, his strides stiffly controlled, as though maybe he wanted to run. Harvey had turned toward the car, one foot on the running board, left arm braced against the car top, head turned to watch the kid.

"So long, Louie."

"Yeah," the kid said. "So long, Harv." He jerked up an arm in a farewell gesture. His arm was up like that, stiff, a kind of Nazi salute, when Stove Harvey killed him. It all happened in an instant.

In the face of cold-blooded murder, Zero was, for the moment, too horrified to move—not that he could have done anything to prevent it with the door between himself and Harvey. Harvey had apparently pulled the automatic, steadied the barrel across his upraised left arm, the movement deliberate and yet so casual in execution that when the blast came it must have startled every man in the car.

It unnerved Walter, the man at the wheel. He let the car jack-rabbit away from the curb almost before Harvey could duck in beside Spig. As for Zero, he had to open the tavern door and sprint at top speed to grab a door handle and hop onto the running board of the car.

Zero looked back at the sprawled and motionless form of the kid on the sidewalk, the right arm extended. A sickening sensation of failure swept over the unseen man who clung to the mobsters' speeding car.

I could have stopped that, he thought. I could have got out there somewhere and kicked Harvey, or jolted his arm. I could have done *something* if I only had known….

CHAPTER 18
WINNER TAKE COVER!

PETE FLOSSO'S Moon River Casino was a long low frame structure, one end of which thrust out over the sluggish water, supported on piles. The most pretentious thing about it was the neon sign in the parking lot. The sign at this last dark hour of the morning was out. A little light showed through round windows like portholes in the two blue-painted front doors.

Flosso's Packard and one other car were parked on the gravel when Stove Harvey's black Caddy rolled in.

"Give me a lead," Harvey whispered as he opened the car door. "You guys don't start anything till I and Spig get through the door."

Spig whimpered, "Stove, Pete'll kill me. He'll kill me!"

"Naw, what you worried about?" Harvey hauled the trembling lunger out of the car. "I'm goin' to take care of you good." He got a left-handed grip on Spig's arm and started toward the blue doors.

In the car, Walter said, "Hell, Harv's in a mood, ain't he?"

"We got to stick by him now," Dutch Willie said. "It's been a long time building. This is it. The big pay-off. This is where the winner takes all."

The blue doors were locked. Stove Harvey kicked at them. Finally somebody came up on the other side.

"We're closed up for the night."

"Stove Harvey. Tell Flosso I got to see him."

179

Then, as the footsteps retreated from the door, Stove Harvey chuckled. "What you shaking for, Spig? You got ants?"

Spig didn't say anything. The footsteps came back, the bolt was pushed open, and Moran, the ex-pug, opened the door.

"Hi-yah, Harv," Moran said.

"Moran," Stove said, and he pushed Spig on into the entry-way, past the yawning and empty hat-check booth, on into the big barn-like room with its tables, its dance floor, and band stage. There were three men at one of the tables, drinking.

Pete Flosso in a white linen suit, black shirt and black tie, was back of the bar, pouring a drink for himself. Somewhere in the building a woman laughed shrilly.

Harvey walked the trembling Spig up to the bar. Harvey and Flosso studied each other, their eyes dead-center, unblinking. Flosso moved finally, brought up a bottle of rye from under the bar and a couple of shot glasses, which he pushed toward Harvey and Spig.

"On the house," Flosso said, showing bright teeth in a studied smile.

Harvey had stopped within a yard of the bar. He shook his head slowly back and forth.

"I don't drink with you." The smile left Flosso's face.

"You killed Ivy," Harvey said tonelessly. "Didn't you?"

Flosso poured himself a drink, carried the brimming glass to his lips without spilling a drop. When he'd put the glass down, he said:

"I been called a lot of things, Harv, but not dame-killer like that. Nobody ever said that about Pete Flosso."

Harvey, without taking his eyes off Flosso, jerked his head to indicate the lunger on his left. "Spig says so. He seen you."

Spig opened his mouth, a dry mouth. "Dud-dud-don't!" his tongue fluttered. He backed off a pace, his hand coming up in front of his face.

Pete Flosso pulled a gun from under the bar with his left hand, fired twice at Spig. Spig crumpled over, both hands clawing at his chest, hit the floor. It was suddenly very still in the room except for a hideous burbling sound coming from the floor.

Flosso, white except for two spots of red beneath his cheek bones, said, "I got myself a damn liar, Harv."

HARVEY TURNED slowly, his eyes still on Flosso.

"You mean you got yourself an eye-witness," Harvey said. He walked toward the entryway, taking his time, showing his broad back to Flosso and to the men at the table. He walked by Moran and toward the blue doors, his left arm up, hand flat to push open the door. He even pushed it a little, then spun on the ball of his left foot, his automatic cradled across his left arm.

It was the same trick he'd pulled on Louie, with this difference—the distance was greater, and Pete Flosso was ready for anything. The shot smashed a bottle on the back-bar. Flosso dropped behind the mahogany, shouted:

"Scatter, you dummies!"

The three men at the table scattered. Moran went for his gun, but was dropped in his tracks by a slug from Stove Harvey. They poured through the blue doors—Walter and two more of Stove Harvey's men with guns in their hands. They fanned out from the entryway, snap-shooting at heads that showed around overturned tables, drawing fire in return.

A light fixture shattered, let down a tinkling rain of glass on Stove Harvey's head and the back of his neck as he ran at a crouch toward one end of the bar. Across from the bar, glass was hacked out of a window by the barrel of a submachine gun.

The cigarette traveled across the room—and stamped itself out in the ash tray!

Dutch Willie, manning the sub, drew a crooked dotted line from one end of the bar to the other, looped the line on a lower level, exhausted his slugs on the bar, saw one of the Flosso men reeling toward him, blood all over his chest but still firing haphazardly.

Dutch Willie threw the empty machine gun at the man, caught him in the head, floored him. Dutch Willie got a leg up and over the sill, burned a Flosso man down with a slug from a hand gun, came on into the room, dived for cover behind an overturned table. And there was somebody there already, somebody dying.

A woman was screaming horribly. A man was screaming like a woman. Somebody was bawling and praying. A single light bulb shed tarnished rays on gunsmoke that layered the air. Dutch Willie straightened slowly. The moaning of the Flosso man behind the table was bothering him, so he stopped all that with a shot at close range that smashed in the back of the guy's skull.

Dutch Willie looked around, toward the bar. Stove Harvey came into view lugging something limp and bloody—Pete Flosso. Stove Harvey pitched Flosso away from him and onto the floor, cursing Flosso.

Dutch Willie said, "Just you and me, Harv."

Harvey looked about dazedly. There was a cut on the side of his face that seeped blood.

"Walter?" Harvey asked. "Micky?" He moved over to where a man lay across the legs of an overturned chair on the floor—a brown felt hat, brim uppermost, lying in front of him. There was blood in the hat, a hole in the front of the band.

Harvey spat nothing; his mouth was too dry. "Walter," he said. "Damn you, Dutch, you ought to saved Flosso for me." He turned and looked at Flosso, and Flosso was moving. He wasn't going any place, but his legs were churning slowly.

"I guess I saved him for you, Harv," Dutch said. "Tough, ain't he?"

Harvey grinned. He walked back to where he'd left Flosso. Flosso was breathing noisily, his legs still working. Harvey pulled out his gun.

"I got one slug left," he said. "I got *the* one slug left." He stuck out a foot and gave Flosso a push. "Hey, Pete," he said. "Pete, I got somethin' to show you."

Flosso lifted his head a little. His eyes rolled up. But nothing else moved at all.

"Drop it, Harvey! Fast!"

Harvey whipped around and wasted his one shot on a voice—a voice that seemingly came out of thin air. Then, too late, he saw the gun that was covering him nosing around the edge of an overturned table.

Dutch Willie poured three slugs into the table top before the other gun spoke once. Dutch Willie's right leg twisted crookedly under him and he went down swearing. Dutch Willie's gun spilled out of his hand as he fell.

"All right, Harvey," the voice from the table said. *"Hands way up and over against the wall."*

Harvey raised his hands slowly, stared at the gun which floated upward, moved to the right. Just a gun. Nothing else. A gun that kept eyeing him as it shifted over toward the spot where Dutch Willie was lying and then floated down a ways.

Dutch Willie's gun tipped up from the floor, butt-end first, stood on its muzzle, then lifted four feet off the ground. There were two guns now, about fourteen inches apart, suspended in space.

"You didn't actually suppose I'd hide back of that table, did you, Dutch?" Zero asked ironically. He hadn't, of course. He'd simply crouched alongside of it, in the open, the gun in his right hand, braced against the edge of the table. *"Not much sense in hiding something from you that you can't see, is there?"*

Dutch groaned, which was understandable. A shattered kneecap is a groaning matter. He might never be able to walk normally again.

"You're going to fry, Harvey," Zero said. *"You and Dutch. Flosso, too, if he lives."*

Harvey watched the two guns maneuver to the end of the bar where the telephone was. The gun on the left side went down on the bar. The other one-eyed Harvey the same as before.

The handset was lifted a little way and the 'phone dial chattered. Then the handset was lifted higher than the gun, and the voice of Zero said:

"Police headquarters, please."

CHAPTER 19
UNSEEN WITNESS

CAVANAUGH NOTICED the guns on the bar of the Moon River Casino as he and his men trooped into the room. Just two automatics lying there on the mahogany, and across from them, against the wall, Stove Harvey standing with his hands in the air and blood pouring out of a cut on his cheek. It was queer. But then there was so much that was ghastly—the stench of death, the cries of the wounded, the hysterical weeping of a woman crouching on the floor, rocking a dead mobster in her arms—that Cavanaugh momentarily passed over what was queer.

After he'd put handcuffs on Stove Harvey and had listened to the fragmentary sentences of Pete Flosso's last statement, Cavanaugh remembered the guns on the bar. He looked for them again, but there only was one.

That was queer, too.

Cavanaugh went to the blue doors to prop them open for the two interns who carried out Dutch Willie on a stretcher. And as

Cavanaugh started back, he heard his name spoken softly from the open door of the Casino office.

"Cavanaugh, will you step in here a moment?"

Cavanaugh paused. His hand started toward his gun.

"Don't, please," the voice said. *"Dutch Willie tried it, Cavanaugh. I don't think he'll ever be the same again, do you?"*

Cavanaugh saw a gun on Pete Flosso's desk, saw it lift, apparently of its own accord, from the plate glass surface.

"Come in, Cavanaugh. I want to talk to you."

Cavanaugh took a deep breath and stepped into the room.

"Close the door, please."

Cavanaugh closed the door, saw the gun wave toward a chair. He sidled over to the chair and sat down like a man with spoiled eggs in his hip pockets.

He said, "You're Zero."

"Yes. And you owe me a little something, Cavanaugh," the deep resonant voice went on.

"I noticed Harvey when I came in," Cavanaugh said with a slight smile. "He looked pretty silly. Thanks for covering him until I got here." He added, "I feel pretty damned silly, myself."

"You owe me about five minutes," Zero said. *"In all common justice, you owe me that much. I didn't kill Steve Rice."*

Cavanaugh nodded. "That's what Ira Rice said. Ira alibied you." He laughed harshly. "How you can alibi a man you can't see, I don't know. But he did."

"Just as easily as you can take a man you can't see into court," Zero retorted. *"But about Steve Rice. Was there a complete post mortem*

examination, or did the coroner conclude that the fall from the roof garden killed him?"

Cavanaugh said, "Steve died of a skull fracture."

"But he fell," Zero persisted. *"He wasn't pushed. There was no one in the penthouse who could have pushed him. He fell, once, in the living room, and hit his head on the fireplace fixtures."*

"Who turned over the furniture?" Cavanaugh wanted to know.

"He did," Zero said. *"You see, I've got a slight advantage over you. You admit that no one could have been in that penthouse with Steve except Captain Zero. But I know that I wasn't there. So I have to conclude that Steve was alone, that he wrecked that room all by himself, and eventually fell over the parapet of the roof garden all by himself and then died."*

Cavanaugh's eyes narrowed. "He purposely set the stage so it would appear that there was a struggle?"

"Not at all," Zero replied. *"He was having a convulsion. Did you ever see a case of atropin poisoning? I have, in the—in a hospital. It took three orderlies to hold the victim in bed. He was like a guy on a blind raving drunk, running into things, falling.*

"So you might look for atropin."

"Thanks," Cavanaugh said dryly.

"And this massacre here tonight—it was a set-up, a deliberate attempt to pit Harvey against Flosso. There were others: a heist on a creep joint that Ivy operated for Harvey, an attempt by Ivy to get Flosso to kill Harvey. She wasn't trying to throw one over for the other, she was trying to get rid of them both. But for somebody else. I don't know who—maybe Johnny The Turk."

CAVANAUGH SAID, "Divide and conquer—is that what it is?"

"*That's what it is. The attempt on the part of one man to get control of the whole town.*"

"Where's Johnny Akara?" Cavanaugh asked. "I tried to have him picked up, but he's vanished. Both Johnny and Joe Venetti are gone."

"*I don't know,*" Zero said with a trace of impatience. "*I don't have a lot of time, Cavanaugh, and there's so much to cover. Lee Allyn didn't kill Ivy Lindhorst, though if you gave him a chance he might be able to tell you who did.*"

"I'd like to give him the chance," Cavanaugh said grimly. "Where the hell is he, since you know all the answers?"

Zero hesitated a moment. "*You may need Lee Allyn to get a first degree murder conviction on Harvey. Both he and I witnessed the cold-blooded killing of a kid named Louis on Canal Street early this morning.*"

"I don't make bargains," Cavanaugh warned. "With you or anybody else, Captain Zero."

"*You still need Lee Allyn,*" Zero argued. "*He's got something else. A notebook.*"

"Belonging to Johnny The Turk Akara," Cavanaugh broke in, smiling thinly. "You see, we're not exactly invisible, but we do make some progress in our own orthodox way."

"*A notebook,*" Zero went on, unperturbed, "*and an I.O.U. payable to Akara and signed by George Manning. I think Allyn might turn these over to you if you'd cooperate a little.*"

"I don't make bargains," Cavanaugh repeated. "If Lee Allyn didn't kill Ivy, what was he doing at her house?"

"He was drugged," Zero said carefully, realizing how thin the ice was. *"He was supposed to get a story from Ivy—something for his newspaper. Somebody had doped Ivy's gin. You can get confirmation on this. Ask Fairish at the World office. Or ask Doro Kelly."*

Cavanaugh winced slightly. "I'd like to do that, too."

Zero, who had not missed the detective's pained expression, demanded, *"What do you mean?"*

"I mean I don't know where she is. She's been missing now for close to thirty-six hours." Cavanaugh saw the gun tremble a little.

"Akara—" Zero began, but Cavanaugh was shaking his head.

"We can't find Akara, I told you."

"What time is it, Cavanaugh?"

The voice had changed, Cavanaugh thought. There was a tightness about it, and it had risen in pitch. Cavanaugh looked at his watch.

"Four-thirty," he said.

"Then listen: Lee Allyn can help you. He was with Doro Kelly—"

"I know that."

"—and he'll help you find her. I know where he is. But you've got to give me your word of honor, Cavanaugh, that you'll go there by yourself, as soon as you're through here, but not any sooner. Is that too much to ask?"

Cavanaugh stared thoughtfully at the space where he thought Zero's head was. "No," he said. "I guess not. Where do I go?"

The gun had started to move. It left the desk, began circling

Cavanaugh. The detective, fascinated, followed the gun with his eyes, saw it approaching the door of Pete Flosso's office.

"On Canal Street," Zero told him. *"A place called Dutch Willie's. And now if you'll get up and open the door for me, and walk straight out into the main room, I'll be much obliged."*

Cavanaugh got up, went to the door, opened it, and walked out. When he was twenty feet from it, he glanced over his shoulder.

He didn't see anything. There wasn't anything there.

Thirty seconds later, when a wild-eyed cop came in with the story that Pete Flosso's convertible had started up and rolled out onto the boulevard with no one at the wheel, nobody believed him.

Nobody but Cavanaugh. And he didn't say anything.

The sun had just climbed over the horizon when Lee Allyn came down the stairs at Dutch Willie's place and crossed the deserted bar to the front door. He looked out through the filmy glass, saw no one in the street. He opened the door.

Ed Cavanaugh's tall spare figure appeared around the corner of the building. He stood, wooden-faced, looking at Allyn. Allyn's eyes blinked behind thick-lensed glasses.

"Why, hello," Allyn said foolishly.

"You're under arrest." Cavanaugh laid a hand on Allyn's arm.

"Now wait just a minute," Allyn protested. "Just a second, Cavanaugh. I've got certain evidence that you might be—"

"Yeah, I know," Cavanaugh said dryly. "And I got a warrant. We'll go pick up that evidence you've just admitted you're illegally withholding, and—in case you've forgot—you're still under arrest."

CHAPTER 20
DEAD MAN'S PITCH

L EE ALLYN paced to the door of his cell and yelled, "Hey, Cavanaugh!"

He was getting hoarse yelling hey Cavanaugh. There had been nearly twelve hours of it. He paced back to the iron cot and kicked the leg of it. His toe was sore from kicking the leg of that cot.

If they had questioned him, if they'd put him into the sweat box and turned the lights on him and questioned him, that would have been better than this. He was being ignored. They were letting him rot.

Cavanaugh had taken everything that Allyn had to offer—the notebook and the Manning I.O.U.—and he had given in return one tray of sub-standard food for a noon meal. Nothing else.

What the hell was Cavanaugh doing, anyway? Didn't his dumb Irish brain realize that it was now nearly forty-eight hours since Doro Kelly had disappeared? Anything could have happened. Anything.

The scuffle of feet in the corridor of the lockup brought Allyn back to the door. Some old paunch in a uniform was approaching, not Cavanaugh. The old paunch stopped in front of Allyn's door and fiddled with keys.

"What is it?" Allyn demanded. "Am I sprung? Can I get the hell out of here? Where's Cavanaugh?"

The old paunch said, "Keep your pants on, son." The lock opened. "Cavanaugh wants to see you, Allyn."

"And bro—ther, it's mutual!" Allyn stormed as he was led out of the cooler, past the desk sergeant, and up a flight of stairs to a door designated as POLICE LABORATORY. The old paunch steered him into the lab.

Cavanaugh was there, standing beside a boxlike contraption of dull black painted metal sheets, open at the front and resting on a wood counter. Cavanaugh looked sick with tiredness, his eyes deep in his angular face. On the stage of the boxlike thing was a narrow slip of paper—the Manning I.O.U.

"Good lord, are you just getting around to *that?*" Lee Allyn was furious and incredulous at the same time.

Cavanaugh looked at the little blond man, mildly surprised.

"I got around to it," Cavanaugh said, "about thirty minutes after I got my hands on it. When she got me on the 'phone that night, Doro Kelly asked if we had any ultra-violet equipment in the laboratory."

" 'U.V.'" Allyn said excitedly. "Well, what about it? What gives? Make with the ultra vi, Cavanaugh."

Cavanaugh picked up a burning cigarette from the counter, puffed on it.

"Since that time," he went on in his monotonous voice, "I've got every available man out looking for Doro Kelly. Then I rushed the D.A. for an exhumation order on Steve Rice's body. On top of that, we had a departmental shake-up. Yancy resigned.

He realized, I guess, the brand of heat he'll have to take when Stove Harvey goes on trial.

"So," Cavanaugh sighed, "we got a new chief of police. He's not worth a damn today, because he hasn't had any sleep."

Allyn shot a pale glance at Cavanaugh. "You, huh?"

Cavanaugh nodded.

"Have they posted Steve Rice's body yet?"

Cavanaugh kept on nodding. He stared curiously at the pale man in front of him. "Steve Rice died of a skull fracture." He waited as though he expected some kind of a reaction from Allyn. When there wasn't any, he said, "If Steve had stayed off that roof garden for a few minuter longer, he'd have died of something else. Atropin poisoning."

Allyn said, "I don't give a damn. Have you found—" He was afraid to ask; he'd been putting it off.

"Doro Kelly?" Cavanaugh shook his head. "No." Flatly and tiredly. "I want to show you something, Allyn. So that you'll understand." He left the sentence up in the air, turned, touched a switch that let current into the ultra-violet lamp above the black stage.

ALLYN STARED at the I.O.U. The slip of paper was literally covered with signatures. There were six of them besides Manning's, and part of a seventh. Two columns of signatures. Somebody named Smith, a Harold Wheeling, a Bruce something or other and—*Doro Kelly*.

Cavanaugh was saying, "The I.O.U. is a phony, get it? It looks like somebody got out a petition, got a lot of signers, in order to get the signature they wanted—Manning's. The others were bleached out and the I.O.U. form printed and filled in. Then Manning was killed, and this was to be presented to his family for collection.

"Doughnuts will get you dollars that the Irwin and Cordray killings were the same thing. Whoever it was—and it looks like the combined effort of Akara and Joe Venetti—They had a neat little murder racket. Find some young sport who is a known gambler, fix up a phony I.O.U. from a signature on a harmless looking petition, kill the sport so he wouldn't be able to deny having signed it, collect from his family. Those kind of folks would rather pay up on a thing like that than have the scandal go into court.

"That's the pitch, but where it ties into the rest of this mess, I'm damned if I know."

"You don't?" Lee Allyn blinked at the new police chief. He pointed to the I.O.U. "That represents working capital for a new organization that expects to take over where Harvey and Flosso left off—as of this morning. It takes money to pull off a power-grab. You've got to buy votes, bribe public officials, pay off the ward heelers. You've got to buy gunmen and terrorists. Ask Ira Rice how it's done—he'll tell you volumes. He did it before. It took money then."

Cavanaugh took a long breath. He nodded morosely. "But we can like it this time," he said. "We're in on the ground floor. If it wasn't for *that*, I'd feel pretty damned good." He tapped Doro Kelly's signature that showed up on the fake I.O.U. "See what I mean?"

Lee Allyn didn't answer. A wave of cold fear passed over him.

"I mean," Cavanaugh was saying, "we don't know how much Doro knew. If she knew, for instance, that her signature was on this thing, she might remember signing a certain petition. She might remember the person who offered that petition to her. If she does, then she knows too damned much for her own good. And that's why we can't find her."

Allyn's hands clenched. "Dammit, Cavanaugh, let me out of here!" It was almost a sob.

Cavanaugh shook his head. "Huh-uh. I told you I've got every eye on the force peeled for her. You couldn't help." He put a hand on Lee Allyn's arm, but Allyn jerked away, cursing. Cavanaugh nodded at the old paunch, and the two of them closed in on Allyn, got him by both arms, shoved him out the door and on down the steps.

A tall thin man dressed in gray turned away from the sergeant's desk as Allyn and the two police passed on the way to the lockup.

"Just a minute there, Cavanaugh."

Cavanaugh paused. Allyn and the old officer paused. Cord Selmer took jerky strides away from the desk, his gray eyes snapping.

"I thought maybe they were holding you, Allyn." Selmer's smile was tight, mirthless. "Don't worry, my boy, I'll have you out of here in an hour. I'll get the best lawyer in town."

Allyn said, "Make it snappy, Mr. Selmer." He looked over at Cavanaugh's wooden profile and grinned. "See? I got friends in the right places. You want to make it tough for yourself, that's okay by us, isn't it, Mr. Selmer?"

Cavanaugh didn't look at Allyn. He said, "Don't waste your time, Selmer. I'm holding this man on suspicion of murder, and I'll go right on holding him until hell freezes over."

Selmer frowned. He put a thumb up toward his mouth, then dropped his hand to his side. "You've got to have a grand jury indictment to do that," he said. "Don't you?"

Cavanaugh said, "Maybe I'll get one, Selmer. Until that happy day, you go right ahead and try to spring Allyn. I'd just like to see you."

Cavanaugh and the paunch wheeled Allyn around and marched him back to the lockup. They had to use force, getting Allyn back to the cell.

"You sap," Cavanaugh said quietly through the grill after the old cop had turned the key in the lock. "You trying to end up in the morgue, like the rest of the guys who know—who *knew* too much? Like Steve Rice, maybe? I'll give you ten to one they've got your name on their little black book right now."

Lee Allyn sank onto the cot, mumbling, "I don't give a good damn." Meaning just that. For if that was where he must eventually find Doro—in the morgue—nothing mattered to him anymore. Nothing at all.

Cavanaugh turned away, a strange bright glint in his eyes....

CHAPTER 21
LADY KILLER

THE BIG man at Mrs. Parsley's front door handed her a white slip of paper which she did not immediately look

The sheer weight of the dog, as it sprang, knocked Joe to the sidewalk.

at. She had not yet gotten over the start the sight of him had given her. It was his size—six feet tall and as broad as the door, she estimated—and the white painted cane in his hand, and the fact that he stood with his head down and his hat pulled over his eyes.

"My lands!" she had said when, at 10 P.M. she had answered his knock at the door. And she was still thinking, My lands! The poor fellow is blind. And him so big and husky like, and yet so puny-fied because he can't see.

Finally, she looked down at the note in her hand, read the typewritten lines.

Dear Mrs. Parsley:

It appears as though I may be in jail for some time, and I would like this man to have the use of Blackie until I am free. Please deliver Blackie to him and oblige.

Your roomer,

Lee Allyn

"Well," said Mrs. Parsley. "Well, indeed!"

Blackie, muzzle at the crack of the parlor door, did some extensive sniffing, and then emitted a low growl.

"Of course," said Mrs. Parsley, "it *is* his dog, and I suppose he can do without him. But won't you come in, mister—um?"

"No, thank you," said the man. "So warm, I'll just wait out here. If I may have the dog, please?"

Mrs. Parsley said it would take a moment to put on Blackie's harness. She went back into the parlor, troubled by grave and probably groundless misgivings.

Just because he's got yellowish hands, she thought. Big, blunt, hairless yellow hands. Some sort of a foreigner, she guessed. She sniffed.

Blackie sniffed, too, all the while Mrs. Parsley was dressing him in his harness. Blackie sniffed, and his great plume of a tail didn't wag.

Blackie doesn't trust foreigners, either, she decided. For all it's supposed to be one world. "But you're Mr. Allyn's dog, Blackie," she said. "Plague take that boy, anyway!"

She walked Blackie, or Blackie walked her, out into the hall and to the door.

"There you are," she said. "Bye-bye, Blackie."

The big man put his yellow hand on the leather covered stanchion. Blackie was bristling and apprehensive, yet large and powerful as he was, he could afford to be open-minded about strangers. He let himself be led down the porch steps and onto the sidewalk.

Mrs. Parsley, watching from the door, wondered if they furnished typewriters to prisoners in the police lockup. Probably, she decided, for newspapermen. They do so pamper jailbirds anyway, now, a body was better off nowadays doing life for a murder than he was trying to make a living and buy food and pay taxes and all....

A block from Mrs. Parsley's house, the big man threw his white cane into a convenient trash barrel. He pushed up his hat, and the light from the street lamp fell aslant his shiny rimless glasses. He was moving swiftly, now, without actually seeming to hurry.

Blackie, having had no exercise for over twelve hours, was eagerly taking all the leash that was given. Down Ash Street to Main, across Main and then west for a block and down South

Newcomb, and a block farther on were the blue lights of the police building.

The big man slowed down, dragging back on the dog harness. Blackie sniffed uneasily, sent a baleful glance back over his shoulder. His lip curled a bit, showing a bright saber-like fang.

A car came into South Newcomb at the corner beyond the police building, and the big man urged the dog forward. This was the part of the scheme that required audacity, and Johnny The Turk Akara would have felt somewhat better about what he was doing if he had known exactly why he was doing it.

But then, he consoled himself, the boss was one very smart man.

It was perfectly timed. The slow moving car was directly opposite the police building at the same moment that Blackie and Johnny Akara arrived between the blue lamps. Then Akara simply released the dog, stepped to the curb, and sprang into the car. The car immediately accelerated.

Blackie stood there for a moment as if he, too, were puzzled. Then he lowered his long snout toward the sidewalk and sniffed. His tail gave a tentative wag. Blackie turned, climbed the steps of the police building, sniffing his way. He stood at the door, tail waving slowly, yellowish eyes brightly alert.

After a moment, the big dog moved over to the side of the entrance and lay down, with a sigh, on the broad top step.

JOE VENETTI was stationed diagonally across from police headquarters and on the ground floor of a deserted store building, the windows of which were covered with posters.

Joe Venetti had been there a long time, looking out through a wide tear in the poster. Being that close to the police made him nervous, but, on the other hand, he got a certain enjoyment out of it—being practically under the noses of the men who were looking for him. He didn't like the job he was going to have to do, but he did understand how essential it was. He was well armed with a gun, a short length of lead pipe, and—*a toy water pistol filled with thin white paint.*

The big dog worried Joe more than the man Joe would not be able to see.

Midnight went by, then one o'clock. The black dog waited patiently on the steps of the police building. Two o'clock came. Joe waited and watched, too nervous even to yawn. Two-thirty. Joe began to wonder if, for once, the boss had guessed wrong.

"I gotta get out of here before daylight," he said to himself. "I'll go nuts if I don't. I'll t'ink I'm a damn' freak inna circus!"

Three o'clock, the dead quiet of dark morning.

The desk sergeant on night duty came out onto the steps of the police building and stretched his arms over his head. Stretched and yawned, noticed the huge black dog with a visible start. He said something to the dog. The dog stood up and wagged its plume of a tail. The sergeant looked pleased. He stooped a little, one hand on a knee, the other extended, fingers snapping, trying to coax the dog nearer.

The dog moved, but diagonally down the steps, ignoring the sergeant entirely, and then trotted off down the sidewalk.

"Hell!" Joe Venetti said. The short hairs at the back of his neck prickled up. He stepped over to the door of the deserted building in which he had been hidden. His nervous hands fumbled with the lock, got it open. He waited only until the sergeant had withdrawn into the building, then stepped out into a street deserted except for himself and the dog.

And one other person.

The dog was trotting north on Newcomb, and Joe followed, his left hand in his pocket on the grip of the water pistol, his right holding the short length of lead pipe. He had rehearsed the boss's instructions over and over in his mind. Get close to the dog, as close as he dared, pull the water pistol and let fly with white paint some of which ought to spatter this Zero guy, mark him, make him a target. Then Joe would use the lead pipe. Or, that failing, he'd have to risk shooting his gun.

One block, two, three, and Joe had shortened the distance between himself and the dog to about one hundred feet. And then the dog stopped in its tracks. Joe, momentarily disconcerted, stopped, too. The dog was standing there, tail wagging slowly, head up and attentive. And then the dog turned, facing Joe, and began retracing its steps.

That's fine, Joe thought. I just gotta wait here. It's better than walking.

But was it better? The dog's trot had changed to a long easy lope, as though it knew where it was going.

"Yeah," Joe said under his breath. "It's after me, dammit!"

He turned and ran blindly back to the corner, then into dark Adams Street. Now, looking back over his shoulder, he saw the dark shape virtually upon him. Joe threw the lead pipe, missed the big beast by a yard. He turned, reached for his under-arm gun with fingers actually numb with terror.

The dog sprang, fangs bared and slashing, the sheer weight of its body knocking Joe to the sidewalk. The gun went off somewhere, clattering, and Joe was helplessly trapped, the jaws of the dog at his throat.

"Easy, boy," somebody panted.

"Don't—don't let it—don't—" With the weight of the beast pinning him to the concrete, with the snarling threat of those jaws at his throat, Joe was not exactly articulate.

"No, Blackie. Not—yet," the voice of the unseen man said, not giving Joe any assurance. *"I've got him now. Got his gun. Over here, boy. Watch, get it? Just watch."*

Joe's indrawn breath came as a sob as the dog moved off of him. Joe's own gun was staring him in the face, and beyond that he saw only the pale night glow of the sky. Unseen hands were going over his body, turning his pockets inside out.

"What's this—a water pistol?" Zero laughed dryly. *"Filled with paint, eh?"*

Joe saw the white stream tongue out into the gutter.

"Not a bad idea, Joe," Zero said. *"Not bad at all—if it had worked. Your idea? I doubt it. Now, if you'll get up—and stop shaking. You're going to get us a taxi, just for you, and Blackie, and me. And do you know where we're going, Joe? To wherever they've got Doro Kelly. You'll give the address."*

Joe got to his knees, felt the gun nosing his spine, saw the black shape of the dog patiently waiting.

"I—I don't know nothin'," Joe stammered. "They don't tell me nothin'."

"You'd better know, fella," Zero's voice said grimly. *"Or I'll tear you apart and feed you to Blackie."*

DORO KELLY came into the half-world between sleeping and waking, and somewhere a bell was ringing insistently. Or maybe that was part of a dream. Like a telephone bell, yet not like it, ringing incessantly.

There was a telephone in this room where they had been keeping her. When first she had noticed it—after that first potent dose of drug had worn off—she had thought, How perfectly careless of them!

But the 'phone had no dial.

When she had experimentally lifted the receiver, a voice had spoken to her. "Miss Kelly, I want to know what you have done with Akara's notebook and the Manning I.O.U. I advise you to tell me—"

She had dropped the receiver, realizing with a cold stab of terror that she recognized the voice at the other end of the wire. There had been no attempt to disguise it.

That meant one thing. They intended to kill her.

There had been food on a tray at the side of her bed when she had awakened. Food that was drugged. She had had nothing to eat after the first time, knowing what they were trying to do. They were giving her something to try to break down her resistance, to make her answer their questions.

"Who is Captain Zero?" was one of them, spoken over the 'phone. And she didn't know. Then they had dropped that, suggesting perhaps they had found out for themselves, or that they no longer feared Zero.

But Akara's notebook and the I.O.U. still bothered them....

She sat up in the bed in the tight little room where the windows were boarded on the inside with pine. The 'phone on the nightstand was ringing.

"Oh, shut up!" she said wearily. She got up, so that she wouldn't be tempted to answer, and saw herself in the mirror, her blue evening dress wrinkled, torn at the bodice.

The 'phone kept on ringing, wearing a path across her brain with its noise.

Finally, she picked up the receiver, just to stifle the thing.

"Miss Kelly—"

"Go to hell!" Miss Kelly said flatly.

"Miss Kelly, I cannot give you another opportunity. Where is Akara's notebook and the I.O.U.? As much as I regret it, I shall have to kill unless you answer."

"You heard what I said." Her voice quavered a little. "I don't know. If I did, I still wouldn't tell."

She hung up. She sagged down onto the edge of the bed, her hands gripping the edge of it until her knuckles were white.

This is it, her mind told her. Stop that shaking. You've been expecting it, haven't you?

Came the clicking of a key in the lock, the rattle of the knob, and the door opened. Johnny Akara stood there, and the gun he was holding was dwarfed by the hugeness of his fist.

He said, "Come on," quietly. "It's too bad."

Yes, isn't it? she thought. Killing me is just killing you, I suppose.

SHE STOOD up and moved toward the door, trying to

be sedate about it, in the dress that she'd slept in. Trying to be courageous when her insides were quivering.

"Please, don't touch me," she said.

"Now, now." And he touched her, took hold of her bare arm above the elbow. He led her out of the room, down a hall that was like any other upstairs hall in an old-fashioned house. Bedrooms opening off of it, a bath, a linen closet. Very ordinary, commonplace surroundings in which she rode a wild nightmare.

Down steps that were varnished oak stripped with taupe carpet, across the waste space that served as a reception hall, through a tall door into a library. Old books on shelves to the ceiling. A broad window with heavy gold drapes, the darkness beyond, her own pale face staring at her from the glass.

And beside the desk stood Cord Selmer—the thin and the taut—a burning cigarette flattened between thumb and forefinger.

"It's too bad, Miss Kelly, that you're not more inclined to be cooperative," Selmer said. As though he meant it. As though it really was too bad.

She stared at his gray, intelligent eyes, wondering what could make a man like that. Jealousy, perhaps? Had he been jealous of old Ira Rice because Ira was top man in the town? Rebellion against circumstances which had given Ira the Selmer Drop Forge on which he'd founded an industrial empire?

"You haven't changed your mind, Miss Kelly?"

"Changed it?" Her laugh was short, on the verge of hysteria. What mind had she to change? What mind was there left to her at this last critical moment?

Selmer's shoulders jerked in a shrug. "It's out of my hands, then. Take her out somewhere, Akara, and do it."

Akara hesitated. "Where's Joe? Couldn't he—?"

"No," Selmer broke in. "Joe is trailing Captain Zero. He is, unless something has gone wrong."

"Something has gone wrong." The resonant voice filled the room. In there with them. Zero.

Selmer whipped around, thin hips plastered to the edge of the desk, his gaze jumping from one inanimate object to another, crossing the glass pane of the window, fastening itself on a gun that seemed floating in space between himself and one of the voluminous gold drapes.

Akara fired. The gun that had no visible means of support leaped and whirled in the air. There was a startled oath that came out of space as the gun struck the floor. Akara poured shot after shot into the area the sound had come from, drowning out Doro's terror-shrill scream.

A dull red stain spread over the surface of the gold damask drapery. There was the *splat-splat-splat* of blood dropping onto the floor.

Doro tottered. A wave of blackness swept over her....

CHAPTER 22
DARK DAWN

"YOU GOT him!" Cord Selmer said, his voice trembling. "Johnny, you got him!"

"I guess so. I guess maybe I did." Staring at the blood on the drape, Akara lowered his gun, lowered it to his thigh. Something closed on his wrist then, wrenched his right arm backward and up. There was a snap like a dry stick breaking, and Akara screamed.

His gun—but *his* no longer—swept up and came crashing down to the back of his skull. Akara pitched forward, fell. The floor trembled. Selmer stepped away from the desk, stood swaying, his hands clenched, his lips pulled back from his set teeth. His eyes wavered between the gun that Zero had turned on him and the blood on the drape.

"That's your pal Joe, back there." Zero said, his voice not entirely under control. *"I had to do something with him when I heard your footsteps a few minutes ago. He was unconscious, for some reason, so I put him back of that drape. He's tied to a hook.—Here, don't try that!"*

Selmer had put his hand into a jacket pocket. He brought it out again hurriedly, faced the unseen man. He ran his tongue over his dry lips.

"What are you going to do? What can you do?"

"Turn you in for murder," Zero said, calmly now. *"You poisoned Steve Rice, right after the meeting at the Community Building. I was standing close to you and Steve at the time, in the parking lot. Steve had suggested a drink, had told you he had a bottle in his car. You said you rarely indulged, but this time you'd break the rule.*

"It was Steve's bottle and he would naturally offer it to you first. You took the drink, and put atropin into the bottle. You'd already set the stage so you could convincingly refuse a second drink. And it was the atropin that killed Steve."

Selmer's lips quirked in a smile. "Skull fracture, you mean.

There's a technicality there, Zero, that I think you've overlooked. The atropin didn't get him."

"*You got a break there,*" Zero admitted. "*Make it attempted murder. But killing Ivy was something else. After you'd used her a couple of times to play Harvey and Flosso against each other, you finally had to kill her. You knew she wasn't to be trusted. And also because neither Harvey nor Flosso had nibbled at the bait of two previously set traps. If you could convince Harvey that Flosso had killed Ivy, you had it made.*

"*And when you shot Ivy, remember, I was there. An eye-witness, don't forget that.*"

"You didn't see anything." Selmer didn't sound as though he was too sure about that. "You couldn't have."

"*I heard a great deal,*" Zero told him. "*I heard what I at first thought was a faucet dripping in the living room, where no faucet could be. That little habit of yours, Selmer—you know what you do when you're in deep thought? You snick your thumbnail across your front teeth, and it sounds a whole lot like a dribbling faucet. That's what I heard. And there's one thing more, Selmer. You know who I am, don't you?*"

"Lee Allyn," Selmer said.

"*And you know because you also realized that Zero was in Ivy's house that night. Zero was there, yet Lee Allyn was the man seen leaving the place in the morning.*

"*I'm afraid it's all washed up now. Akara will talk. He'll tell the whole thing to save his own skin. It's—*"

ZERO BROKE off. The big window behind Selmer was

shattered by a blow from a gun butt. Cavanaugh, alone, put a leg over the sill and stepped into the room.

"Okay, Zero, I'll take it from here." Cavanaugh moved toward Selmer, a pair of handcuffs open and waiting.

Selmer tossed a clenched hand up to his mouth, at the same time throwing his head back. Cavanaugh sprang at him. A small glass bottle fell to the carpet. Cavanaugh kicked Selmer's legs out from under him, spilled him to the floor, got legs astride Selmer's thin neck, tried to get his hand into Selmer's mouth.

"No—good," Selmer gasped. "I got it. All of it."

Cavanaugh clamped the bracelets on Selmer, then straightened away. He scooped up the bottle Selmer had dropped.

"Atropin," he snapped. "You don't give a damn how you die, do you, Selmer?" And Cavanaugh strode toward the desk and the 'phone. Out the tail of his eye he saw something that required a second look. He saw Doro Kelly suspended in space and floating toward a couch against the side of the room. He saw Doro descend, slowly and gently, to the cushions.

Cavanaugh snorted. "I brought your clothes, Allyn. They're outside in my car. You can go any time you want."

"How's that? What did you call me?"

"Allyn," Cavanaugh repeated. "You left your prints on the safe in Steve Rice's apartment. Zero's prints, that is. Then after I'd picked you up this morning, I found Lee Allyn's prints matched. In the cooler tonight, after you'd pulled that vanishing stunt, I knew you were still in the cell."

Cavanaugh jabbed at the 'phone dial. Waiting, he said, "I deliberately left the cell door unlocked, knowing you were in there. I needed your help.... Hello," into the 'phone. "Cavanaugh speaking. Send the boys out to Cord Selmer's place on Belleview Road. And—" he glanced at Selmer sitting on the floor, his hands manacled—"oh yeah, the ambulance—for a boy full of atropin and another full of lead."

He hung up, swung around.

"What are you doing, Allyn?"

"Kissing her. You can tell her I kissed her."

"Ha! Like hell I will!"

"Then I'll tell her next time I see her." Zero started toward the door, paused there a moment. *"Incidentally, Cavanaugh, what about you and me? Who else knows who I am?"*

Cavanaugh said, "Nobody at headquarters. I haven't told anybody. And I don't intend to." His smile was small, but it was a smile. "I figure you and I ought to kind of work together."

"Partners, huh? In just about everything except—well—you know what I mean."

Cavanaugh glanced at the unconscious girl on the couch. He didn't say anything, didn't make any promises. But he knew exactly what Zero meant.

POPULAR HERO PULPS AVAILABLE NOW:

THE SPIDER
☐ #1: The Spider Strikes $13.95
☐ #2: The Wheel of Death $13.95
☐ #3: Wings of the Black Death $13.95
☐ #4: City of Flaming Shadows $13.95
☐ #5: Empire of Doom! $13.95
☐ #6: Citadel of Hell $13.95
☐ #7: The Serpent of Destruction $13.95
☐ #8: The Mad Horde $13.95
☐ #9: Satan's Death Blast $13.95
☐ #10: The Corpse Cargo $13.95
☐ #11: Prince of the Red Looters $13.95
☐ #12: Reign of the Silver Terror $13.95
☐ #13: Builders of the Dark Empire $13.95
☐ #14: Death's Crimson Juggernaut $13.95
☐ #15: The Red Death Rain $13.95
☐ #16: The City Destroyer $13.95
☐ #17: The Pain Emperor $13.95
☐ #18: The Flame Master $13.95
☐ #19: Slaves of the Crime Master $13.95
☐ *NEW:* #20: Reign of the Death Fiddler $13.95

THE MYSTERIOUS WU FANG
☐ #1: The Case of the Six Coffins $12.95
☐ #2: The Case of the Scarlet Feather $12.95
☐ #3: The Case of the Yellow Mask $12.95
☐ #4: The Case of the Suicide Tomb $12.95
☐ #5: The Case of the Green Death $12.95
☐ #6: The Case of the Black Lotus $12.95
☐ #7: The Case of the Hidden Scourge $12.95

G-8 AND HIS BATTLE ACES
☐ #1: The Bat Staffel $13.95

CAPTAIN SATAN
☐ #1: The Mask of the Damned $13.95
☐ #2: Parole for the Dead $13.95
☐ #3: The Dead Man Express $13.95
☐ #4: A Ghost Rides the Dawn $13.95
☐ #5: The Ambassador From Hell $13.95

CAPTAIN ZERO
☐ *NEW:* #1: City of Deadly Sleep $13.95

OPERATOR 5
☐ #1: The Masked Invasion $13.95
☐ #2: The Invisible Empire $13.95
☐ #3: The Yellow Scourge $13.95
☐ #4: The Melting Death $13.95
☐ #5: Cavern of the Damned $13.95
☐ #6: Master of Broken Men $13.95
☐ #7: Invasion of the Dark Legions $13.95
☐ #8: The Green Death Mists $13.95
☐ #9: Legions of Starvation $13.95
☐ #10: The Red Invader $13.95

DUSTY AYRES AND HIS BATTLE BIRDS
☐ #1: Black Lightning! $13.95
☐ #2: Crimson Doom $13.95
☐ #3: The Purple Tornado $13.95
☐ #4: The Screaming Eye $13.95
☐ #5: The Green Thunderbolt $13.95
☐ #6: The Red Destroyer $13.95
☐ #7: The White Death $13.95
☐ #8: The Black Avenger $13.95
☐ #9: The Silver Typhoon $13.95
☐ #10: The Troposphere F-S $13.95
☐ #11: The Blue Cyclone $13.95
☐ #12: The Tesla Raiders $13.95

DR. YEN SIN
☐ #1: Mystery of the Dragon's Shadow $12.95
☐ #2: Mystery of the Golden Skull $12.95
☐ #3: Mystery of the Singing Mummies $12.95

MAVERICKS
☐ #1: Five Against the Law $12.95
☐ #2: Mesquite Manhunters $12.95
☐ #3: Bait for the Lobo Pack $12.95
☐ #4: Doc Grimson's Outlaw Posse $12.95
☐ #5: Charlie Parr's Gunsmoke Cure $12.95

www.ingramcontent.com/pod-product-compliance
Lightning Source LLC
Chambersburg PA
CBHW020415180626
46812CB00003B/986